Hope

Hope

S. J. Wilkins

CURRAWONG PRESS

Currawong Press books are available exclusively through
Deseret Book Distributors
57 West South Temple
Salt Lake City, Utah 84101

Author photo by Bethany Smith

ISBN: 978-1-59992-904-0

To my family, both the living and the dead

The spirits of the just are exalted to a greater and more glorious work; hence they are blessed in their departure to the world of spirits. Enveloped in flaming fire, they are not far from us, and know and understand our thoughts, feelings, and motions, and are often pained therewith.

The greatest responsibility in this world that God has laid upon us is to seek after our dead. The Apostle says, "They without us cannot be made perfect" (Hebrews 11:40), for it is necessary that the sealing power should be in our hands to seal our children and our dead for the fulness of the dispensation of times—a dispensation to meet the promises made by Jesus Christ before the foundation of the world for the salvation of man.

Joseph Smith

Acknowledgments

Many Church leaders and members have influenced my attitude and feelings toward the gospel, but three in particular deserve acknowledgement for their remarks because of their significant influence on the development of *Hope:* Elder Dallin H. Oaks for his talk "The Challenge to Become"; Elder Jeffrey R. Holland for "Cast Not Away Your Confidence"; and President Joseph Fielding Smith for "Seek Ye Earnestly the Best Gifts."

I must also thank others who inspired me with their personal thoughts and experiences about the relationship between temple work and missionary success, and the miraculous involvement of ancestors in our family-history work. I believe these thoughts have helped to crystallize one of the key relationships and objectives in this narrative. Thank you.

I should like to express gratitude to my editor at Walnut Springs Press, Linda Prince, and her boss, Garry Mitchell. Thanks for believing in this project. Finally, thank you to my long-suffering family, who patiently stood by as I wrestled with the task of creating and finishing this work over some fourteen years. You *do* deserve medals. I am also grateful for the many people who have peered into the writing and offered thoughtful response. Though I do not name each one of you, you have all had an effect. However, I must thank my mother for being willing to proofread the manuscript more than just a few times, and my wife, who has no doubt read it more times than she can remember.

Prologue

My name was Isaac. In my early years, when I reflected on the meaning of my name, I was reminded of the Old Testament, of Abraham and of the challenge of sacrifice, and the great character traits of humility and faith. As a consequence, I grew up believing I must always live a good and noble life. I wanted my children to know I believed this principle. And I suppose it was this very fact that led to my death.

In the year of our Lord 1837, I became aware of a new and remarkable movement, a new religion brought to Queen Victoria's England by a small group of Americans. The Latter-day Saints—Mormons. Their message was one of power, authority, and the parting and knowing of the heavens. Their message made known the might and majesty of a real, resurrected Christ, the very Son of God preparing a kingdom on earth in preparation for His millennial reign.

Inspired, I desired to join their church, but was prevented from doing so when I was killed while trying to rescue two women and a man from a burning mill. Thus my desire for baptism was thwarted. But, joy of joys, I came to understand that my wish might yet be fulfilled by the living, if my baptism could be performed by someone still in mortality.

Naturally, I considered it best that my family do this for me. But since I was dead, the work of guiding them into the truth presented a significant challenge. And it was made infinitely more so. In the wake of my passing I was accused of maliciously starting the very fire that had taken my life. I was therefore an arsonist, and because others had died, I came to be known as a murderer.

My good reputation was destroyed. My name became taboo, unspoken, my family tainted by their association with a killer. With my memory ignored, my wish for membership in the Lord's kingdom was forgotten.

Yet the truth was that I had become the victim of another man's crime, and the true story behind the fire was kept hidden. A young girl's identity was made secret and my wife and children's shame carefully preserved, allowed to remain because it served a valuable purpose.

Imagine again the pitiable shame of being the murderer's family. Imagine again my grief at knowing this burden was borne unjustly, yet unable to prove my innocence and another man guilty.

The misfortune might have remained forever this way, except, at last, the grief itself created a receptive heart in my youngest son: Ephraim Immanuel Shaw—Manny. Thus it was that we received our second opportunity.

Manny had been born with a remarkable gift—a powerful spiritual talent. And even in the aftermath of all that had happened, his gift lay only suppressed. His was an innate and childlike strength: the discerning of angels and ministering spirits.

There was, of course, a danger in attempting to reach him this way.

Manny worked in Ormley Mill where the fire had happened. He was employed by a man with whom I had formerly been friendly—a certain Edward Reeve. Some five years earlier, Manny had ventured to express his regret at the suffering his father had caused, and sought permission to apologize in public to the men of the mill. In addition, he sought to understand why the fire had happened at all, and had hoped that Mr. Edward Reeve who was master of the mill, would take pity and help him to see.

But Mr. Reeve's wife had been lost in the fire, and he could never be brought to speak of it. So he flatly refused Manny's request, saying it would be wrong to revisit the past, wrong to speak of the dead, and wrong to dwell on the sins of the father. Mr. Reeve said a person must be possessed with an evil spirit to want to speak of these sins gone with the dead, and everyone concerned would be grateful to him for letting it rest in the past. When Manny protested, insisting he had a right to understand, Mr. Reeve became angry and took up a whipping rope and beat him for impudence.

courtyard, swirling around the burnt-brick walls of the mill. And as he stood quietly there, a thought caught him by surprise. It came softly but there was no mistaking its urgency: *Take up your cross and leave.*

In the stillness of the morning, the idea came into Manny's mind with so much clarity that for a moment he thought someone had actually spoken. He looked around, but from his brother's blank expression it clearly had not been him. There was no one else near them.

Take up your cross and leave? Manny glanced at the mill and wondered. Leave the mill? He looked toward the open, inviting moorland. The impression had been so definite. Was it a warning, an urging?

He considered leaving that morning but felt the danger of changing, and concern at the idea of jeopardizing his mam's well-being. He might not find another employment. If he left the mill like this he might never be allowed to return, Mr. Reeve could be harsh, especially to the men he didn't like.

The thump of his heart increased, the coming unknown pounding up in his throat. No. It was foolish to think of leaving. It was insanity to think he could find another workplace that paid as well. The idea was sheer desperation. True, he hated having to work here, but how could he think of walking away? His mam and Will depended on the income they managed together to earn. In spite of the permanent discomfort of being "Isaac's sons," Reeve paid them well—in fact, Manny knew it was charity, really. Except, he argued, they were made to earn every last farthing. But he could not avoid the reality that this decision would affect his family for the worse. And yet he could not explain why he knew there was so much more to this feeling than just sheer desperation. It was something he knew he would follow.

Take up your cross and leave. The words again, more urgent than before.

What would Will think? Manny knew his brother was impatiently waiting behind him at this very moment, accustomed to this ritual lagging behind. Despite the frequent silences between them, they valued their friendship. Manny knew that, like him, Will merely wished to prove loyal, different from his father, and trustworthy. But Manny also knew his brother believed dreaming achieved nothing. It was sheer hard work that mattered.

And now Will stood waiting, scuffing his clogs against the rutted highway. In this small detail there lay a more recent point of tension: Manny wore not clogs, but boots, a gift from the beautiful young woman who had taught him to read, the ward of an old yeoman farmer who lived on the edge of the moor, just a short half-mile walk out of the village. A girl both he and his brother had been smitten with for years.

He heard Will clear his throat and knew what it meant. They must go in or they'd be late. He looked at Will's impatient face, and his heart began to race at the thought of the impending departure. In his soul, Manny knew he must go far away from this place that threatened his sanity.

The mill window was empty. Mr. Reeve had gone. Manny knew he would have only a minute to persuade his brother to come with him.

Take up your cross and leave.

He wondered if the pounding in his chest would tell in his voice. "We've to leave, Will. I feel it." He gestured at his heart, then saw the shock in his brother's face. "We could all of us move away from the village."

Will looked doubtful.

"I swear I'm going to do it," Manny continued urgently. "We could all of us make a new start."

It was not unusual for Manny to dream, even to be unpredictable, but this strength of resolution, this level of conviction seemed to have taken his brother by complete surprise. For a moment Manny believed he was entertaining the idea. But the hesitancy lasted too long.

Will shook his head, father-like, and walked away toward the mill, leaving Manny standing there alone. A final few weavers jogged away over the courtyard and disappeared into the loom shed.

The trill of a blackbird rose over the silence. Manny looked round to make absolutely sure Mr. Reeve had gone, then took a sharp breath and hurried away.

—∞—

Early morning mist ghosted along the Orm, trailing above the water, rising and twisting. Wide and sleek and almost silent, the river curled through the valley, curved almost to the doors of the stone-terraced cottages sunk tight in the moorland.

As soon as he was beyond sight of the mill gates, Manny ran, his step lighter, his boots crunching against the highway. The village was quiet now, and he could hear the faint cries of sheep on the hillside. He felt suddenly exultant at having acted decisively, felt the thrill of running away. Then he reasoned with himself that he wasn't so much running away as running to something else—something better—running away to take charge of his future. He was improving his station in life, looking for work of his choosing. Even the imminent rain was exciting.

Now at the age of almost one and twenty he wanted to prove himself able, for her sake—the old farmer's ward, the young woman they called Hope. He wanted to give her more than a lifetime of dour, unchanging Ormley. He felt suddenly reckless, free as the gulls wheeling high in the sky above. He knew she aspired to become a teacher, and he wished at least to be her equal. Through the years since Mr. Reeve's whipping, Manny had slowly, relentlessly been made into something he wished not to be. But he knew now that he could and must change himself for Hope.

She had always made him feel he could be a different man than his father had been. Manny was grateful and humbled by her faith in him. And lately, he had been even more so. In the last few weeks, Hope had discovered she was adopted. Her guardian had been unwilling to speak of the circumstances, and Hope, still struggling with the shock of the discovery, had not yet pressed him for details. And so neither had Manny pressed her.

He resolved to try Northwood first. The market town was only a short journey from the village, and there were mills and factories all around the outskirts. It wouldn't take him long to reach them if he ran. There were two roads he could take: the main highway, a simple, rutted road that followed the river; or a higher, less-used road—a narrow, untended hill track. He thought of taking the latter to avoid being seen, and then decided against it. He'd soon be out of the village anyway.

Maybe if he had no luck in Northwood he'd try Manchester, or Stoke, or even London. In any event there must be no going back to the Ormley Mill. Manny unclenched his fists. The breeze felt cool against his skin, and he brushed the palm of his hand against the dry-stone wall beside him. One thing was already certain. He felt happier.

It was at the outskirts of the village that he saw the man—a stranger, walking carefully down the bridle path from the moorland and approaching slowly from the other side of the river. The stranger stepped nearer, a cloth bag slung across his back, a brown book in his hand. It was something about his manner that made Manny stop. The man was tall, and his eyes burned like the sun. Manny wanted to move on, yet felt impressed to stay where he was. The man paused at the bridge. Then he hitched his bag higher on his shoulder, narrowed his eyes, and gazed around at the village as if he were puzzled by it. Their eyes met, and his face filled Manny with light. Then the man turned and hurried away.

Manny was so surprised at the intensity of this vision that for a moment he forgot why he was leaving the village. He ran, calling for the man to wait. But the stranger strode faster as if he regretted being seen.

"Wait!" Manny called again.

The man stopped abruptly and looked back, seeming anxious not to linger.

"Who are you?" Manny asked quietly. Somehow he could not escape an overwhelming sense of awe.

"They call me an elder." The voice was soft and possessed an unusual lilt, and Manny realized with a start that the stranger was an American. "I'm Mormon, a missionary," the man explained. He looked unsure about saying more. Then his face softened. "See here, young feller, I'm preaching later, down over in Northwood—aside the Orm, at the railway bridge on the east of town. My name's Armitage. Why don't you come and listen?"

For a moment Manny didn't know what to say. The prompting he'd experienced earlier had urged him away, and straightaway he'd met this man. The man had filled him with such an intensity of light. And then, though the encounter lasted barely a minute, a feeling of such warmth came over Manny that he knew he must agree quickly. "I'll come," he said. "I know the place you mean." All notions of finding work had left him.

Another rather unexpected idea began to form. Perhaps sooner rather than later, he and Hope could emigrate. Yet regardless of this, he knew she must be informed of the elder's arrival, and quickly.

They were just outside Northwood, as the elder had said. Manny knew the place well and watched the man preparing to address the crowd. Strangers sometimes came through these parts, but this American had gained more attention than travelers usually did. The missionary's strange aura was still noticeable, though not quite as bright as it had been in Ormley. Manny calculated that close to a hundred people had come to listen—perhaps a couple of dozen men, a lot more women, and at least two dozen children. Some people stood on a footbridge; others straggled along the river's edge. A few bystanders, their voices dissenting and mocking, heckled the man on account of his being American, but the elder seemed unperturbed and smiled good-naturedly.

The iron underside of a railway bridge rattled as a train leaving Northwood thundered overhead, its shrill whistle piercing the air. A layer of dust and dirt shook loose from the girders, and the clack of freight carriages faded as the train steamed into the moorland.

The missionary looked up, his face suddenly serious, as if he was ready to speak. The crowd was silent. Somewhere a baby cried out, and then it was hushed.

"Brothers and sisters," Elder Armitage called boldly. His voice echoed back from across the river. "My brothers and sisters, I come to preach a message of peace, of prophets, of a living Christ, of a kingdom of God that can save you. I invite you to be baptized, for it will change you—" He stopped as though interrupted by a sudden thought. "But before I speak of this . . . I feel to tell you that forgiveness springs from understanding. Understanding does not mean approving, nor does it mean granting permission for injustice to continue, but it does allow us to have compassion. In understanding we find freedom, the strength to abandon resentment. Forgiveness grants us the power to possess and then be consumed by our Savior's compassion. And His compassion, my brothers and sisters, is freedom—a freedom from anger, a freedom from hate, and, in the end, the only perfect freedom."

The same thrill of warmth Manny had felt in Ormley washed over him again. He looked around, wondering if anyone else felt as he did. He could see from Hope's face that she was also moved by the elder's words. She stood with her head held high, dressed as she so often was in a high-necked gray calico dress, her black hair pulled back into a neat bun. A few loose strands of hair lay gently against her cheek, her pale skin contrasting the blue of her eyes. Manny felt his heart leap and then guiltily averted his gaze.

She'd seemed just as excited as he'd been by the elder's arrival, and Manny had felt an intense pleasure at inviting her to come with him to the town. He looked at her once more and noticed a tinge of pink on her cheeks. The same light he'd seen in Elder Armitage was beginning to emanate from Hope as well. A sense of peace filled Manny, and he reached out to take hold of her hand. He knew they would both be baptized.

Elder Armitage stood waist-deep in the river, close to the edge where the water was calmest. Manny slid down the embankment toward him, his hands catching against briars. The river was swollen, and driftwood tumbled past in the froth. He made a silent pledge. This baptism would signify a new beginning. He would strive to become a man of peace. "Blessed are the peacemakers,'" he thought, "'for they shall be called the children of God.'"

It was enough. He was ready to commit.

The cold water pushed at Manny's legs and then his belly. He grinned and shivered. The crowd had gathered above him, on the footbridge—some smiling, others frowning and turning away, shaking their heads.

Elder Armitage raised his arm and spoke slowly. "Ephraim Immanuel Shaw . . ."

All became silent as Manny sank under the water, his heart pounding. The river sealed above him, closed over his face. For a moment he lay in the elder's grip, immersed in the thundering water. He felt the current beat at the riverbed, rushing and humming all about his head and arms and legs, his old life rushing away. Then he rose.

Hope was still smiling as she too emerged from the river. Her face flushed as she climbed up the embankment toward Manny, and he felt a surge of pride at seeing her so happy, so alive. Gentle clapping broke out behind them, and the crowd rippled as people moved away.

Manny handed Hope his coat, then helped her wrap it around her shoulders. It was good being so close to her. Even though he was shivering, he felt warm, confident, renewed. He thought of the marriage plans they had laughed at so many times, imagined the bite of salty sea air on the deck of a schooner, the captain performing the wedding.

Now was the time to ask. Gently, Manny took hold of Hope's hand. "Will you . . ." But his heart was racing and he stalled. He couldn't tell whether she knew his intent, but she blushed as she looked up at him, and he saw tears welling in her eyes, her face alight with anticipation.

He wanted to say something more profound, something more eloquent. The words he had prepared seemed awkward, inadequate. "I'd like to ask your guardian a question."

He felt a hand on his shoulder. It was the elder. He was holding a Bible and smiling. "We need to confirm you now," he said, "and bestow upon you a gift—the Holy Ghost."

Manny looked at Hope and saw in her eyes a mixture of disappointment and excitement.

"Come, come with me before you catch your death of cold," Elder Armitage urged. "Come and meet Sister Aitkin." He gestured toward a woman who stood smiling down on them from the bridge. "She owns the lodging house where I've been boarding, and while we're there we can find new clothes for the both of you." He held up his Bible. "We can talk more comfortably there as well. Besides, I have a doctrine I'm longing to share, something that will help you in the future."

⎯⎯∞⎯⎯

Storm clouds rolled in over the moorland, making the late afternoon seem like evening. Will swung his fist again, smashing it against Manny's mouth. "Where have you been, lad?" he spat. "You've been gone all day."

Blood trickled down Manny's chin. He was grateful Hope was not here with him, that he'd agreed to her request that she wait in Ormley. This was not a spectacle he would have wanted her to witness. He wiped his mouth, trying to stop the blood dripping onto the shirt Elder Armitage had lent him. As Will looked disdainfully at the new clothes, Manny swallowed, his breath punctuated by his heartbeat, his knuckles red and swollen.

The brothers stood alone on the rutted highway, just outside the village. Manny clenched his fists, his jaw tight. He'd been surprised that Will had come looking for him, but even more surprised at his brother's response.

"We've done right," Manny insisted. The shock he'd felt at Will's reaction was turning to anger.

"We've found peace. And no one, most of all you, is going to take it from us."

His brother laughed and then stared at him scornfully. "You've been tricked, lad. You should never have left."

"No, you're wrong. I won't go back on this."

"You're sick in the head, lad—that's all there is to it."

They circled each other in silence, stepping over the ruts and stones in the road. Behind them, the storm moved over the village. Thunder volleyed across the moorland, and the cloud split, spewing rain into the valley.

The rain swept over them, drenching the highway. Manny held up his hand to shield his eyes. "Maybe you don't care who lives or dies here, Will. But I swear Hope and I do." He turned, bowing his head against the rain, and hurried toward the village.

Will rushed up behind him and yanked him back. They tripped and fell heavily. "You and Hope?" Will demanded. "You ain't right. Have you no pity for your mam, or me?"

Pushing and pulling at each other, they scraped over stones, slipped in the mud. They had never fought like this, and Manny felt sick to his stomach. "What's happened to you, Will?"

Shaking, he leaned in close, and Manny could smell his stale breath. "It's not what's happened to me, lad. It's what's happened to you," Will whispered. "But you can't run away from who we are."

Manny tried to wriggle loose, but his brother had him pinned.

"You're scared, Will, that's all. You're scared of what I've done. But it could be for the best. And one day, you'll regret you didn't come."

Will looked suddenly weary, resigned, as if overwhelmed by a weight he would never divulge. He turned his head away for a moment and then looked back, determination to hold his family together etched into his face again. "I swear I'll hurt you worse than this if you don't do as I say. Now just you think about our mam. Remember her, will you? And by the way, Mr. Reeve said he'd even increase your wages if you stay. Don't forget it."

Will stood up awkwardly, spat on the ground, and hobbled away.

Manny watched his brother go and grimaced at the throbbing in his mouth. The rain fell heavier, stinging his face. He didn't move even though mud seeped slowly into his clothes. Then the rain ceased as abruptly as it had begun, and the clouds pushed on toward the moorland.

There was the sound of horse hooves and carriage wheels splashing through puddles. It could only be Mr. Reeve; no one else in the village could afford such transport. Manny took a deep breath as he tried to put the turmoil out of his mind and prepare for the inevitable interview. The mill owner's black coach drew closer, and the driver pulled back on the reins. The horses shook their heads, snorting, pawing at the ground. Mr. Reeve leaned out of the window, looking amused. But Manny thought the man also seemed disconcerted.

"Whatever's the matter?" Mr. Reeve asked. "Do you need help?"

Manny winced, pushing himself up, and managed a rueful smile. "No, sir, it's nothing."

Mr. Reeve stared at him. It was clear he did not believe this response, and he looked as if he was trying to read more into the answer. But he only declared, "I'll say no more about it then. And I'll not inquire into the matter of your disappearance this morning. I trust you've seen your brother and that he's conveyed to you my offer?" It was more of a statement than a question and was immediately followed by another. "Do you know if your mother's at home?"

"I expect she will be, sir."

Mr. Reeve touched his hat and smiled. "Then I'll leave you." He looked toward the driver. "Stop at The Fold."

The driver flicked the whip, and the horses clipped away.

Two

In Confidence

At the edge of the village, an awkward lace of black-and-white cottages lay in shadow. The storm had passed over them, and although the sky showed signs of clearing, there were still swaths of gray cloud. The branches of a large oak tree dripped rain, and Manny could hear the frantic gurgle of water gushing into the river. Otherwise the village was quiet. He hid behind the dry-stone wall that ran alongside the road and wondered what to do. A few of the womenfolk were about, and he did not wish to talk to anyone until he spoke with Mr. Alderman. The villagers would doubtless want to know where Manny had been and what he'd been doing, and his disheveled appearance would only make them more curious. If Will's response was anything to go by, news of the baptisms was probably best kept quiet, at least for now.

Manny watched Mr. Reeve's carriage sway as the driver climbed down from his seat. Mr. Reeve had stopped outside Manny's house. The mill owner raised his brass-handled cane and tapped the door with it. The door opened and Mr. Reeve bowed quickly, then took off his hat and stepped inside. There was nothing especially unusual about the mill master visiting Manny's mother, but he couldn't help feeling that Reeve enjoyed exercising his unspoken right to descend upon the villagers whenever he chose, for whatever intent served him best. Manny was never comfortable in Reeve's presence, always doubting the sincerity of mill owner's actions.

Manny edged past the coach and then ran to the footbridge over the river. He hurried across it, and then, confident he was now out of the driver's sight, strode up the bridle path toward the Aldermans' home.

The storm had retreated and the newly freshened air had taken on a copper hue. Above the ridge of rock at the brow of the hills, a fragile shaft of sunlight reached through the cloud and spread over the village. Manny inhaled deeply, filling his lungs and clearing his mind. He held his breath for a moment, enjoying the silence. He'd always appreciated the freedom of the moorland— the clean, damp air, the tug of the roving wind. He breathed out gently, excited about asking Mr. Alderman for permission to marry Hope. But it was not so simple to forget the fight, and Manny felt shaken and badly presented for the request.

Before the moor summit, the bridle path swung right, and he could see Mr. Alderman's farmhouse tucked behind the spinney of oaks bordering the moorland. The wet slated roof glinted in the sunlight. The walls of the house, built of stone from the local quarry, had a certain kind of permanence about them, sort of like Mr. Alderman himself. Manny stopped and stood, nervously rubbing his hands against his trousers as he tried to muster his courage.

Squinting through the sitting-room window, he saw a hunched figure in a chair and stepped back quickly. Mr. Alderman was at home, reading, as he so often did.

Once a wealthy merchant farmer, Mr. Alderman had been a scrupulous man of industry, a man who traded wool and cotton with merchants in America. But his concerns about slavery put an end to his investment in cotton, and for the several years before his retirement he had simply traded wool with the local mills. But even this he did no longer—now he lived in comfortable retreat in the privacy of his farmhouse, with Hope and an occasional housekeeper. There wasn't much Mr. Alderman did more than read. Hope said it made him feel educated and gave him an aura of respectability. He seemed happy to be advantaged and aloof, and this impression was reinforced by his imposing physical presence. His silences were frequently considered by Hope as a disapproval of discussion in general. That said, she had never actually been treated unkindly by him—his philosophy had always seemed to be loyalty to responsibility. His care of her was, to all intent, an employing of this principle. And Manny wondered if the self-important manner the villagers accused Mr. Alderman of possessing was simply a misunderstanding of the man's love of solitude and meditation. He had apparently once been heard to say that so much of his time could now be spent profitably reading books and the newspaper, and that if only he'd had the will to write when he was a young man his entire career might have been so very different. Perhaps there was the spirit of a romantic in him yet.

Nevertheless, this habit of pondering solitude also made the prospect of speaking with Mr. Alderman, especially in the light of the actions of this particular day, an even more daunting one. It was little wonder that Hope was afraid of how he would respond to the news of her baptism, or discussion of marriage.

Manny glanced down at his trousers, regretting the mud smeared all over them, and hoped the old man would not think less of him. He bent down to wipe them clean. But it made little difference, and so, adjusting his shirt, he took courage and marched toward the front door.

Manny sat quietly in one of Mr. Alderman's high-backed armchairs, trying not to muddy the upholstery, even more conscious of the state he'd arrived in.

Most of the stone floor in Mr. Alderman's sitting room was covered by a Persian rug, an item he had claimed to have brought with him from London when he moved north in 1835. Beneath the window, on a mahogany desk, a copy of *Paradise Lost* lay at the top of a pile of scattered books. His fondness for reading meant a weekly excursion to the bookshop in Northwood, and from this shop he purchased books written by a variety of authors as diverse and applauded as Dickens and Brontë or Shakespeare, Chaucer, and Milton. Indeed Mr. Alderman read them all on a regular basis.

A white china vase, centered on the windowsill, reflected the embers of a dying wood fire. But though the fire was low it still warmed the room, and a small pile of logs suggested it would continue to do so well into the evening if Mr. Alderman intended. The sky darkened outside, and rain clattered against the window. Manny cleared his throat and held his hands up to the flames.

Over the mantelpiece, a picture frame held a portrait of Hope. Beneath it, in front of the fireplace where Manny sat, Mr. Alderman faced him. On one of the arms of the old man's chair, the pages of an open book fluttered. Mr. Alderman picked up another log, threw it onto the fire, and then closed his book. Wincing a little, he turned and eased himself back into his chair, his bulky frame straining the seams of his jacket. He seemed tired, yet surprisingly pleased about the baptisms as he asked intently, "So you've both embraced Mormonism?"

The fire crackled, sparks swarming up the chimney. The clock on the mantelpiece chimed. Manny cleared his throat again and tried to smile.

Looking distracted, Mr. Alderman pushed himself out of his chair and walked to the table. "I only wish Hope had come back with you." He placed his book down and tapped the cover with his finger.

"There's more to it than . . ."

"They say they're strange, though," Mr. Alderman interrupted absentmindedly. "Deluded even."

Manny bit his lip. This request might be harder than he'd thought. "She stayed a while in Northwood. She wanted some time before . . . I said I'd ask . . ."

Mr. Alderman turned, looked straight at him, and smiled. "I'm delighted for what you've done. And yet, you don't comprehend the significance of it."

Trying to compose himself, Manny stood up. Hope's all-knowing eyes stared back at him from her portrait. He touched the picture frame, somewhere near to her feet. Hesitating wouldn't help—he must just say it. "It's not what you think, sir. We love each other. I wish I didn't need to ask for credit, but we'll need it for . . ."

Mr. Alderman took Manny's arm. "Yes, yes." He seemed uninterested in Manny's sudden earnestness and just a little troubled by some sudden thoughts of his own. "You are not the only ones who have news." He pulled Manny close and then pointed to the book he'd been reading. It was a copy of the Book of Mormon.

"This elder Armitage came here as well, to the farmhouse." Mr. Alderman glanced toward the window, where the afternoon light was fading. "Come with me."

⸺⚬⚬⚬⸺

Outside, evening hung in the trees. His Book of Mormon in hand, Mr. Alderman was already ahead of Manny, limping quickly away toward the ridge of moorland overlooking the valley. Something about the distraction in his voice unsettled Manny, and he felt a new sense of unease.

Somehow, in his excitement to find Hope, he had not reflected on the fact that he had first seen Elder Armitage on the bridle path leading down from this very farmhouse. Why had the elder not said anything about the visit? Surely he must have noticed Hope's surname was the same as the farmer's. The chance that Mr. Alderman would not have disclosed his own name was extremely improbable. Manny hurried to the old man's side.

"You've spoken to him? But he's said nothing of any such meeting. Where are we going?"

Mr. Alderman raised his hand. "Patience . . ."

The wind knifed across the ridge, cutting through Manny's clothes. He tugged at his coat collar, trying to block out the cold. But it was the chill inside him that discomfited him most.

In the valley, a weather vane gleamed in the dusk light. Farther away to the west, Northwood sprawled beneath the storm. A heron, legs trailing awkwardly, black-gray wings stretched wide, beat its way along the river and on past the mill. Crows cawed from the woods, and the distant sound of barking dogs carried from the other side of the valley. In the past these sounds had always been a pleasant reminder of home, but tonight Manny felt like a stranger. The shadows stretching into the village seemed suddenly eerie, and he was filled with an overwhelming sense of inexplicable melancholy.

Mr. Alderman turned and pointed to an outcrop of rocks and a clutch of trees, far away on the moors. "You see those, Manny?"

He nodded.

"It's where I first learned to pray, near there in the shepherd's hut. It gave me strength when Hope was young. Shepherd's Well is a fitting name for the tarn, I think." He fell silent and stared at the moorland as if lost in a maze of thought. "Manny, God is moving on us here in Ormley." Mr. Alderman opened the Book of Mormon and pointed at some words. "Read this. Aloud."

Hope's guardian had never spoken like this before. Manny felt surprised by his manner and a little embarrassed. But he read anyway. "'For behold, this life is the time for men to prepare to meet God; yea, behold, the day of this life is the day for men to perform their labors.'" He paused, unsure if he should continue reading. The farmer's silence suggested that he should.

"'And now as I said unto you before, as ye have had so many witnesses, therefore I beseech of you, that ye do not procrastinate the day of your repentance until the end; for after this day of life, which is given us to prepare for eternity, behold, if we do not improve our time while in this life, then cometh the night of darkness, wherein there can be no labor performed. Ye cannot say, when ye are brought to that awful crisis, that I will repent, that I will return to my God. Nay, ye cannot say this; for that same spirit which doth possess your bodies at the time that ye go out of this life, that same spirit will have power to possess your body in that eternal world.'"

Manny stared at the words, wondering what Mr. Alderman meant by it all.

"Now listen," the farmer said earnestly. "The next few days may prove dangerous—for Hope and for you. Indeed for all of us, perhaps. But you must not be diverted from your decision to change, to be baptized. You have done right. I've enough assets to help if needs be." He smiled and then squeezed Manny's shoulder. "Perhaps you could even come and work here for Hope and me. I've been thinking about starting up sheep farming again. I could make use of an undershepherd."

"No. It's good of you, but . . ."

"In any case, I'd say keep the news of your baptism to yourself, at least until I have taken care of some now-pressing matters."

"Why?"

Mr. Alderman looked troubled. He leaned forward and brushed moss from the stone wall. "Because the village will shortly be forced to confront its history. We shall all need time to reflect." He seemed to rally himself. "I must go to Hope myself, to tell her how surprised and pleased I am with her choice to embrace the Mormons. Then we can speak more about you both. Where is she now?"

"Northwood." Manny knew he should be glad the farmer had been so receptive, and yet he felt Mr. Alderman wasn't really listening. Because of this, Manny didn't want to broach the subject of marriage, though he knew not doing so would betray Hope's confidence. "West Road, number 13. It's a lodging house belonging to a lady called Jane Aitkin." Manny looked down, pursing his lips. Maybe it would be better if he and Hope both spoke to Mr. Alderman.

"Now, try not to worry," Hope's guardian said. "With luck it'll all be worked out soon enough. But for now, it's enough talking." He stood and stepped back onto the bridle path. "Be sure to come back in the morning. And keep the book."

Manny wanted to protest, but he could only nod his agreement. Mr. Alderman was already walking back to the farmhouse. The idea of asking for Hope's hand in marriage now felt rushed. How was everything going to be worked out if the farmer wouldn't even listen?

"Hope'll be glad to know you're happy," Manny muttered.

He sat for a few hours, delaying the inevitable return home, and eventually found himself standing uneasily on the bridle path, a few yards from the farmhouse. He held the Book of Mormon in both hands, staring down at it. It seemed like a gateway to another world, a threshold that promised to open a whole new vision of who he was. For a moment he didn't quite know what to do, yet he realized it now belonged to him and that in an inexplicable way he belonged to it. Manny placed the book carefully in his coat. He tried to work out what he could say to his mam, wondered what she might say when she knew what he'd done.

The peace he had known at seeing Elder Armitage seemed like a dream, and Manny wished it would return. With any luck, even if Will had told Mam what had been done, news of Manny's baptism would still be limited to the family. Mr. Alderman's warning was unnerving. Why should Manny not say what he had done? He plucked a stem of grass, held it thoughtfully for a moment, and then spun it between his fingers, trying to clear his mind.

He jumped at the sound of a door opening and looked around. Mr. Alderman stepped out of his house, pulling on his coat. Manny waved. Perhaps because it was now dusk, Mr. Alderman hadn't noticed him; indeed the older man seemed lost in thought and walked back inside, leaving the front door open.

All around Manny, the fields were quiet, but for the scuff of his boots and the distant gentle slap of the river against its banks down in the valley. The sudden sound of footsteps behind him made him turn quickly. His brother grabbed him and then laughed. Manny smelled the ale on his brother's breath and pulled sharply away. As he did so he thought he saw another man, away in the woods, watching them, his face obscured by a broad-brimmed hat. When the shape faded into the shadows, Manny wondered if he'd only imagined it.

The woods were deathly quiet, and Manny realized he was holding his breath. He turned back to face Will. He grabbed at Manny's collar and then pulled him back down the bridle path. "This is what you're doing to me, lad," he said hoarsely.

He looked back over his shoulder. "And this is what comes of you meddling in things you've no business with."

They stumbled in silence down the path, and as they neared the footbridge over the river, Will's bearings seemed to have returned. "Mam's fretting," he said as though he'd come for Manny against his will. "I've not told her what you've done yet. I didn't think she'd be able to take it from me. So you'll have to tell her yourself."

The wind trickled through the trees. Manny thought he heard someone laughing. He listened again, his heart pounding in his breath as he peered into the darkness.

"I told you, you're possessed." Will sounded as if he was trying to make light of things. But he also sounded like he was trying to make amends. "What you need is your home, where you belong."

Manny gripped the bridge wall, trying to stop shivering. He attempted to smile through his clenched teeth. He wanted to make peace with his brother, wanted to shrug off the fear that was clutching at him, wanted to receive the friendship Will was offering. But instead he turned back to his brother, his conviction returning. "You're not me dad, Will. I bet he would've listened to me. He wouldn't have let you treat me like this."

Will stiffened. "Don't talk about him, lad. Anyhow, he's not here now, is he? So our mam needs us. Us, Manny lad! And just you wait till you get back to work. Then you'll remember who you need in this village."

Three

Manny's Mam

Without being fully aware of what he was doing, Manny half stumbled, half ran over the cobbles of The Fold toward his house, already bracing himself for the ritual of his mam's unpredictable nerves. If there was one character trait Manny had that would serve him well but make his life a challenge, it was his stubborn determination to keep a promise in spite of any amount of opposition. But he knew this would lead to contention with his mam—an experience he did not relish. He hoped he could speak well, that somehow he could recapture his earlier peace. He thought about how much he loved and respected his mam, how her resilience inspired him. But seeing the apparition in the woods troubled him, and he felt entirely unprepared for the conflict he knew lay ahead. He stopped at the steps to his house, heard Will cursing behind him, and then stepped carefully up to the doorway.

The family's cottage, along with the other half dozen or so homes in The Fold, had been there since before the mill. Once the possession of proud hand-loom weavers, they were now a daily reminder of the onward march of industry and the leftover stones of yesteryear.

On the whole, the villagers in Ormley had adjusted. There had been little choice—the hand-loom industry was in decline. The weavers had to adapt, relocate, or slide slowly into the muddy waters of poverty. So the more forward-thinking embraced the rescuing investment of Edward Reeve's mill and retained their respectability. Manny knew his mam needed her home at the edge of the village, overlooking the fields and the Orm, and knew it would have broken her heart to have been forced to leave it.

A gust of cold air slipped into the kitchen as Manny stepped inside. He wondered if his face would betray how fragile he felt. He forced the fear from his mind and concentrated on the growing sense of relief that he would at last be able to explain his actions.

He heard Will bolt the door behind them, and the shadows from the candlelight suddenly flickered higher on the wall. Manny's mam stared out of the window, into the darkness that shrouded the street, a shawl tied close around her head. She squinted into the shadows, her hunched shoulders more bowed than usual—bowed as if she felt the same weight of unseen jeopardy that Manny felt.

The windowpane misted. He watched his mam scrub the glass more vigorously than the task really required, then step back sharply as if demanding an immediate explanation. That she had not addressed him by name confirmed how upset she was. Manny avoided her piercing stare, but this only made her become more agitated. Her voice was hard when finally she spoke. "Look at me when I'm talking to you."

At first he thought about how he might resist her anger, how he might salvage some calmness in the face of the coming storm. But he could not think and instead was aware only of her straightening to face him, holding her head up proudly. He felt a twinge of guilt, knowing the physical pain this would cause her. If she was ever asked for her opinion about her sons, she swore they were good to her. Her unpredictability was only a reflection of the deep distress she lived in, never speaking of the fire or its circumstances to anyone. Her twisted figure simply expressed her shame, and her posture had grown a little worse each succeeding year.

Manny knew his mam had also been ailing with an ever-decreasing mobility, a malady that had accelerated in the past year. And if that was not misfortune enough, he suspected she was losing her sight. Her movements had become less sure, less fluid—though she would never admit to it. Neither Manny nor Will had raised the subject with her. They'd wanted to protect her dignity and self-respect, and until she made mention of it they declined to do so. In any case, she still retained her mysterious gift of mother sight, able to see things even with her back turned, and in spite of the fact that they were now men, they still deferred to her matriarchal leadership. Their shared weight of shame had driven an understanding deep into their souls. They had developed an unspoken loyalty to each other.

Now that he was home, greeted by the lingering aroma of stewing vegetables and meat, Manny's trust in this loyalty softened his anxiety a little. This room, humble place that it was, was his home, had been his security. The home they'd rescued and built and survived in together—this home that smelled of dust and tallow, this warm kitchen that smelled of mutton stewing in the pot and of his shirts drying in front of the stove.

He took a deep breath and smiled at his mam, trying to rally himself in the hope that a confident presentation of his decision might sway her, that it might show proof he was capable of choosing well. He would be strong. Skulking and trembling on the hillside had been unseemly—he was no longer a child, and he must behave like the man he wanted to be.

But his mam still wasn't smiling, and as she limped toward him, her hand pressed firmly against her back, he could see no way to persuade her to feel differently. She reached forward to take his hand and then clasped his arm. The grip was tight. "I've hardly stopped pacing this floor of ours since Will told me you didn't turn in for work." She looked suspiciously at Manny's clothes, but asked nothing. "Come and sit down. I've saved you some of your favorite." She looked back at Will, who shrugged in moody silence. Then she picked up a bowl of hotpot and shoved it in front of Manny before retreating into the shadows.

"Our William's got good news, you know." Their mam seemed genuinely more at ease, though she still did not smile. "Mr. Reeve said he's to make him an overlooker." She thrust something across the table. It was a gleaming sovereign. "He gave us this as a celebration."

Manny looked at his brother, genuinely taken aback and, if truth be told, a little jealous. It wasn't that Will couldn't do such a job—he could, and he was more than capable of doing it well. Manny was just surprised because there had been no indication that such a job was in the offing. But there again, who could predict what Mr. Reeve would do? Despite his determination to be rid of the mill, Manny felt the pain of another rejection.

"That's good, isn't it?" he said, trying hard to be sincere. He picked up a spoon and stirred the hotpot, pretending to look for the flakes of meat.

"Aye, lad. It was good till I heard you'd happen to run off." Mam's voice was harder now. She frowned at him and leaned forward, staring at his mouth. The blood was gone, but the bruises had given him away. "You've been fighting, haven't you?" She stared, first at him and then at Will, as if seeking confirmation, then back at Manny. "And you, you've done some'at that's got your brother in an uproar. But William won't tell me. He's insisting you must."

Manny's heartbeat quickened, and he realized he was gripping the spoon more tightly than he needed to. Could she be made to understand? Was there any way he might pull off a miracle and inspire his mam to be baptized as well? If only she could feel what he had when he first saw Elder Armitage. She might soften—if he could make her agree to see the American.

"Well, lad, what've you got to say for yourself? William hasn't been hi'self all this afternoon."

There was no easy way to begin. Manny took a deep, deliberate breath and put the spoon gently down on the table. He hoped Will would at least not interrupt. "Mam, I know we've not had it easy. I know we've had to manage on next to nothing. I wanted it to change. I think we need to change."

He tried not to rush the words, but he couldn't help speaking quickly now. "I heard a voice, a feeling. It told me to leave Ormley. And when I did I met a man who helped me. I think I've found a way for us to better ourselves. Some'at to help us."

"He wants to shame you, Mam," Will protested. He glanced at Manny's clothes and sneered, "He's a turncoat. But he hasn't the sense to know what he thinks, or what he's doing, and he's going to shame you and me and hi'self." Will was in full flow now. "He reckons as he's been seeing things, hearing voices. But he wouldn't work today. He ran away." He paused as if for the sake of dramatic effect. "And then he went and joined the Mormons."

Manny turned in time to see his mam's look of shock.

"I reckon he thinks he's going to leave the village with Hope Alderman," Will said scornfully.

Manny thought his mam might be sick. She had turned away from him and was clutching at her throat. "Tell me this isn't true!" she wailed.

"Mam, I can't. I've been baptized. I know it were the right choice."

Will came striding across the kitchen, and Manny braced himself for another outburst. "So, what are you going to do now?" his brother shouted. Spit sprayed from his mouth. Manny tried to turn his face away but Will had it, squeezing it between his fingers. And then his brother started to laugh, mocking him. "He reckons he can change. He reckons he's above us."

Manny shoved his brother away and stood. "Why?" he shouted. "Why's it wrong for me to want to change? I'm sick of the shame of what me dad did. I can't stand being here in this house, being forced to remember it every single miserable day."

His mam and brother looked as shocked as Manny felt. He hadn't meant to say those words. He hadn't even been thinking them. For a moment there was complete silence. Manny tried to pick up his bowl of stew, but his hands were trembling so much he didn't take hold of it properly, and he knocked it instead. The bowl hit the floor, scattering vegetable and meat across the kitchen. There was silence.

Manny clenched his fists, his shoulders and stomach tight. He was on his family's side, but they couldn't see it. Still, he knew he had to say more. "No. I've had it with the mill, Mam. We're more than this. We need to get out." He was imploring them now, with an unexpected surge of confidence. He sensed the tension in the room but looked defiantly at his brother, daring him to try to stop this outburst. Will glared back at him, and Manny thought for a minute there might be another fight. But then his brother looked away.

"I'm sorry," Manny began. "I don't want to hurt you. But I have to follow this feeling."

Ignoring him, his mam wiped up the stew and walked slowly to the stove, the hotpot dripping across the floor as she went. She refilled the dish, and the ladle clanked against the pan as she threw it back into the pot.

"I saw an American," Manny said gently. "I saw that he were shining, he were filled wi' light, on the Orm Bridge."

"Your father . . ." his mam gasped. She seemed to be struggling with something awful, forcing herself to speak. "Your father nearly joined the Mormons. Have you no shame?" The effort to speak of the past was clearly causing her immense pain. "It caused the fire . . . the mill fire . . . and everything else."

Nothing his mam could have said could have shocked Manny more. His desire to become a Mormon had brought back the uncomfortable fact of his father's crime, with all of its horrendous associations. It had, after all, been this very fact of Manny's life that had created his desire to change. He was dumbstruck.

"Here, Manny," his mam said. She wiped away a tear and thrust the bowl of stew at him. He wanted to ask questions, but her face was set. There would be no more discussion. She held out the bowl again, and Manny knew she was trying to make amends for the argument. "Be a good lad." She almost managed a smile. "You didn't know . . ."

It was as if the previous few minutes had never happened. Her face was softer now, more composed.

"But . . . then . . . if Dad . . ." Manny protested. He wanted to ask questions, could see the surprise in Will's face too, but he fell silent, knowing it would only hurt his mam if he pressed her for answers. Manny tried to keep calm. But his mam wouldn't look at him, so he reached out and took her arm. She was shaking.

Manny began to think about his encounter with the missionary, trying to regain some composure of his own. He heard himself saying, "He spoke of forgiveness. It was a message for us, for me. I believed him. I thought his coming could bring us all happiness. I didn't want you to be ashamed, or afraid. And Mr. Alderman said . . ."

The mention of the old farmer's name had a similar effect as the mention of Manny's baptism, except this time it was only his mother that reacted. The significance of confiding in Mr. Alderman had clearly passed over Will as it had Manny. His mam instantly put her finger to her lips, indicating that she wanted him to stop.

"What's that man got to do with us? Don't talk of him. He's not to be trusted. He could ruin us all with his meddling." She was staring intently at Manny as if struggling to maintain her composure. "Now listen to me. You've been tricked. I know you meant to do right—you wanted to help." At last, she managed a smile and tugged at her shawl. "But believe me, Manny, the Mormons. . . ." She shuddered, leaned forward, and whispered hoarsely, "Mormons are from the devil." She fumbled with her hands and made to stand up. "Look at me, Manny. Look at us, lad. We need your wages. We all need each other. What's the good of William's new work if you leave us? That's what the Mormons'd put into your head— to leave us. We'd never see you again."

She took a deep breath and carefully smoothed her hair, then reached over and smiled again, tenderly stroking Manny's cheek. "There lad, it's over, but oh what a commotion it caused."

"If . . ." he began.

But she wasn't listening anymore. She was more interested in returning her kitchen to a state of order. Manny sighed and knelt down to help pick up the last few pieces of carrot and potato on the floor.

"Never mind the mess," his mam said kindly. "Just run along to bed. We've had quite enough upset tonight. Look at us . . ." She flicked at the hotpot that was still on her dress and then shuffled toward the staircase.

Manny stared wearily at the half-empty bowl of food still in front of him and listened to his mam's labored coughing as she climbed the stairs.

Will was staring out the window, his back to Manny. When his brother finally turned around, Manny could see he was making an effort to be agreeable. "Think on it," Will said in a strained voice. "Without your wages we could end up lost, condemned to the workhouse. You couldn't do that to us, Manny, could you? If there's a Mormon God, he'd understand what people need, wouldn't he? It's not too much to ask for a house and health, is it?" Will was reaching out, offering to shake hands and to be resolved. "I'm sorry. You were right—I were scared. I'm scared about making Mam suffer. You understand that?"

But Manny didn't reply. He couldn't help thinking of the way the events of the day wove together, and he began to suspect they were more than mere coincidences. Oddly, he now felt elated to have discovered something about his dad, and though he could not think how, Manny was convinced there was significance in what had happened. He knew he must remain faithful to his commitment in spite of the conflict it would create. At the same time he understood exactly what Will meant, and knew instinctively that if he remained true to his convictions he was going to lose the association of his family. There was nothing he could do to make them see. Nothing he could say would make the slightest difference to their views of what he had done. He reached out to shake hands, but he knew it would be wrong to leave any room for doubt with regards to his commitment. "I don't know what to make of what Mam said. But I won't—I can't—back down on this, Will. I know what I felt, even if it is confusing now."

His brother turned away. "Suit yourself. I'm going out. I need a drink." He left abruptly, pulling the door shut behind him.

Manny felt a wrenching regret at the prospect of facing a future without his family, and was troubled by the thought that he was jeopardizing their safety and well-being. Yet he knew again that in spite of his best efforts to be happy, if he did not change he would eventually go mad, and they'd lock him away. It would amount to the same thing in the end. The weight of the choice drove him onto his knees, and he was compelled to pray. He wasn't exactly sure how to, nor did he quite know what to say, but the very act of seeking brought him peace. He heard his mam's footsteps as she paced the bedroom above. He wondered what she would say if she saw him like this. He blew out the candle, and the kitchen fell into darkness. Then Manny closed his eyes and concentrated, trying to shut out the room, trying to find a sanctuary.

In his mind, he saw Hope, as clearly as if she stood beside him, her face shining like an angel. They were stepping toward each other in a shadowy copse, the moorland silent behind them. Softly he took her hand, drawing her fingers to his lips. The whole world seemed to stand still. But Hope pushed him away and ran into the trees, the woods closing around her. Before Manny could call her back, Mr. Reeve was there in a coach, sweeping through the woods, reaching down from the driver's seat, leering, mocking, and taking Hope away. And then they were gone.

Manny opened his eyes in a rush, sweat beading on his forehead. He felt empty, unsettled by the darkness and the unexpected vision, felt the loneliness and the forbidding silence of the kitchen. The thought of losing Hope to Mr. Reeve surprised him, left him wondering at the stability of his mind.

He shook his head, trying hard to reject the strength of the vision. It was all anxiety—it was fear. He must learn to face up to it. He forced his mind to clear. Then, as he knelt in the darkness, awareness began to emerge in his mind, a sense of future things and a gradually rising sense of elation.

One day he, Manny, would be a father, and what he chose would affect his children. Will and his mam were not the only ones who had claim on Manny's help. Thousands of lives would be forever affected by what he chose now. No matter what the future held, he must go forward. He must be strong. There was nothing for it but to go on, with Hope, in good faith.

Manny wondered what his mam would do when they discovered him gone. He picked up his coat and quietly made for the door. He must speak with Mr. Alderman again, as soon as possible. There were so many things to organize. And, of course, Manny must still seek permission to marry Hope. He cringed at the thought that he had been so slow to come forward. But little could be done about that now. As for sleep, the idea of getting any soon seemed remote. There was far too much to think about.

$\mathcal{F}$ *our*

Another History

Hope sat down at Sister Aitkin's kitchen table, feeling mostly happy. She wondered how Manny had fared with her guardian. It seemed odd that he had not yet returned, and she quelled the concern lingering in her mind. She glanced around at the room where she had just been invited for supper. It was a smaller, more lived-in room than the cold, lonely parlor where she had been sitting all afternoon, and much more modest than the kitchen at home. Her guardian had developed a fine taste for china, and the shelves had become filled with various plates and cups from all over the world. It was a strange quirk of Mr. Alderman's character, and it made him feel traveled.

But in spite of the differences and the privileges Hope had always enjoyed, she had learned to be well-mannered and gracious. On the whole, she was an amiable young woman, eager to please, and quick to express gratitude.

She was well-liked on account of being temperate and thoughtful, though beneath her calm and agreeable disposition was a notable capacity for courage and independent will. Oddly enough, her decision to remain away from home was both out of character and predictable. In short she was, as her recent history had revealed, a bit mysterious. It was little wonder that both Will and Manny were so taken with her.

The kitchen was almost dark now, lit only by several flickering candles, the wax slowly gathering at the bases. Above Hope's head, a line of shirts stretched across the room, hanging close to the stove. They sagged just above the hot plate, absorbing the greasy steam that rose from the frying bacon. For a moment Hope's thoughts turned to the future, and she imagined what life would be like when she and Manny had a home of their own. She knew his thoughts despite his failure to communicate them earlier, and she wondered where they might finally live, how they would survive, how they would prosper. It was all so exciting to consider this new beginning—her chance to finally reach maturity, to show that she was ready to take her place with other mothers.

But there was something else, something she had not told Manny before he had gone back to Ormley. At her baptism, as she stood in the river, she had sensed profoundly the presence of angels. She had felt another person's companionship— warmth and love unlike anything she had ever before experienced. Perhaps, she thought, her mother. No one else knew it, but this feeling had been the cause of Hope's joyous smile on emerging from the water.

Thus her mind returned repeatedly to her baptism, and then to the moment Manny had first come to her, breathless and full of excitement, bearing the news of a mysterious traveling missionary. The whole event had been a whirlwind, and Manny had inspired her with his confidence. There had been a light in his face that she had not seen before. He seemed so sure, so full of faith—quite different from the haunted young man he sometimes was. And Hope had known as well, that herein lay her fate. For a moment, she had imagined America.

The shock of her recent discovery that she had been adopted still left her cold. Sometimes she was unsure how to refer to the man she had always called Father, yet there was no reason to question his decency. Although she wouldn't admit to it, she knew her running away was unfair, and her decision to stay away left her feeling ashamed. But the memory of Manny striding away to speak with her "father" thrilled her. He would need to be persistent. She knew that her father (there was nothing for it but to give him his due title), a private man, had rarely talked about his feelings, let alone hers or anyone else's. But in spite of his reluctance to talk about such things, he needed to know that at the responsible age of eighteen she felt quite old enough to know what she wanted, especially in view of what had lately been disclosed about her past. And her guardian must hear from Manny that he loved her. Perhaps her father would be troubled by their particular request to be married in the manner they had chosen. It was so hasty—there was no disputing the fact. It was likely to be nothing short of a scandal. People would talk. They all thought Hope such a refined and proper young woman. Marrying in such circumstances . . . and marrying such a person. But her mind was made up. She knew it was acceptable in the sight of God, and this much strengthened her.

She brought her mind back to her new friend. Sister Aitkin had removed a pan from the hob and now peered at the bacon before putting the pan down again. She was, Hope thought, a pleasant woman—plump and cheerful, given to a refreshingly direct manner of speech.

Sister Aitkin picked up a knife and stooped over the table to cut the loaf. Then she straightened, a lump of bread in one hand, the knife in the other. "So you plan to be married at sea, then?"

Hope blushed. "Yes, if my . . . if my father will advance us the credit we require for the tickets."

"Won't he object?"

"Well, you see . . ."

"Won't he care about you just running off like that?"

"Well, yes, I suppose he might." Hope felt unnerved by how much she suddenly wanted to say to this woman she barely knew. Perhaps it was her host's own directness that encouraged it. It was welcome, however unusual it seemed. "I'm not sure," Hope went on. "But, you see, I'm adopted. I found out a few weeks ago. And I've longed to know who my parents were. My guardian won't speak about them. He's a private man and won't tell me. I'm not sure he even knows." She blushed, wondering if Sister Aitkin would think her improper for being so forthright.

Hope's host seemed distracted by the spitting bacon. She turned away quickly and pushed the pan to the side of the hob. Fixing Hope with a wry smile, she gestured to her heart. "I reckon a person should always do what's in here." She skillfully skewered the meat and laid it out on the plates in one smooth movement. "Shall we ask a blessing on this?"

Hope nodded and bowed her head. She was accustomed to her father saying grace at each meal, but it felt different to listen to this Mormon offer a sincere prayer of thanks for what was before them. She was also humbled to hear Sister Aitkin express appreciation for Hope's and Manny's recent baptisms.

They ate in silence, and when they had finished, Sister Aitkin folded a piece of bread and wiped around the pan with it. "You and 'im sure it's the right thing to do, though? Choosing to run off just like that?"

"Well, you see, Manny's desperate to get away from Ormley. He doesn't speak about his father's death, but I know he's haunted by it."

Sister Aitkin busied herself with her food, apparently trying to resist the impulse to ask further questions. But Hope felt compelled to explain.

"No one speaks of it much, but Manny's father set fire to Ormley Mill, and then died there."

Sister Aitkin was silent. She looked embarrassed, as if she wished she hadn't asked.

Hope blushed again. There had been too much said; it was all too indiscreet. "Anyway, going to sea is a way for us to get married." She carried her plate to the sink. "We need only find one that will take us to Ireland or somewhere close by, perhaps even the Isle of Man. We don't need to go far. We'll find a ship with a captain who's willing to marry us, go to sea and be married, and come back to the village as man and wife." She smiled at the thought of it.

"Oh, that's good," Sister Aitkin said quickly. Then she added, "That you'll come back. I mean, it'd be a shame for us to lose you so soon."

Hope was flattered by Sister Aitkin's friendliness. Her earlier concern had diminished, and now her confidence increased. "But I think Manny wants to go to America. He says he'll be able to earn enough to send his mother money as well." Hope felt a thrill of excitement at the thought of going to Liverpool, of finding a ship, of committing themselves to the journey to the New World.

"Well, I think it's lovely," Sister Aitkin said, squeezing Hope's arm. "The idea of going to sea to get married, that is. And I hope your guardian sees just how in love you both are."

"Now that we're decided," Hope said brightly, "we want to go as soon as we can. It is better we do. You see, I fear Manny's brother believes he loves me as well."

Clearly surprised, Sister Aitkin started to laugh. "Oh. Well, in view of that, you're welcome to stay here as long as you wish." She looked at Hope and seemed suddenly motherly. "If you'll take my advice now, though, what you need is a good night of sleep. And if you don't mind my asking you, if there's still no sign of Manny in the morning, I'll put you to work on some errands. I think you'd find our Tuesday market a pleasant place to visit while you wait for him to return. Though I must say I'm surprised at how long he's taking to return."

Hope nodded her agreement and then looked away, wondering if her own disquiet showed.

The next morning, she stood at the edge of town where the road from Ormley joined the turnpike. It was odd that Manny had still not returned, and she was at a loss to understand the delay. She lingered in the pale morning sunlight, watching the mothers and children streaming into Northwood and toward the market. She suddenly felt a sense of belonging with these strangers and wondered how she could leave it all behind, how she could think of leaving it to go to another land. People traveled from all over to buy and sell here. This bustling market town provided an exciting contrast to the quiet of Ormley. It wasn't that she didn't love solitude, for she did. But there was also a desire for change, a yearning deep in her soul for an understanding of who she was, of why she had become an orphan. The conversion to Mormonism had helped satisfy some of this, but she still longed to know the identity of her parents.

Although Manny had still not returned, Hope felt sure her father would help them. She thought for a moment about buying him a gift to say thank you, and then decided against it. She should wait and do this with Manny—after all, they would soon be man and wife. They must learn to think about and decide on such things together. She smiled at the thought of taking hold of her future, of beginning to live as she chose.

But the morning wore on and there was still no sign of Manny. Hope waited until she heard the chime of the church bells and decided to go back to the lodging house. Sister Aitkin would be waiting for the groceries.

The main road through Northwood was bent and twisted, and it split the town along its center. Wagons and stagecoaches clattered past Hope, with the sound of horses' hooves and the jingle of brass. The rattle and clip of wheels and hooves clashed with the steam engines that rolled, clanking and whistling, into the station. All along Main Street, drapers, boot makers, cobblers and iron mongers advertised their wares. Everywhere there were many and various shops, yet they looked almost squashed, as if they had been outgrown by the large and numerous taverns lining the road.

A police station with its own magistrate's court dominated the north end. Smog hung everywhere over the market. Mothers called to children who scurried and darted around butchers' and bakers' stalls. The smell of raw meat, and cabbages, of coal smoke and drains wafted across the road. A few clerks hurried along the street, while market traders rubbed their hands and called into the sulfur-laced air.

"Candles, a dozen an ha'penny!"

"Bread, get your bread 'ere!"

Three older men, their leathery faces weather burnt, lingered outside a tavern door and nodded a greeting, respectfully touching their hats as Hope passed them. Two whippets ran circles in front of her, barking and yapping, and she smiled graciously, acknowledging the old men's greeting. At the north end of the market, at the foot of the police station, West Road curved away like a rib. She hurried down it, back toward the lodging house, the noise from Main Street fading behind her.

Later she sat, still waiting, watching diligently from the parlor window. But there was no sign of Manny. Hope rose from her chair and stepped closer to the window, where she pressed her face to the glass and tried to see to the end of the street. Why had she not returned with Manny? In her heart she knew the answer, though she would not yet admit it to herself. Her pride and self-respect had been hurt by her guardian's reticence to speak of the circumstances that brought her into his care. Had she truly been adopted? He would say nothing of these things. Running away was a protest against his unfairness. She was a woman who would now make her own way in life. But she knew they must be reconciled, and in spite of it all she did not bear him ill will.

Her long-sleeved gray dress was fastened up to the collar. Her breath felt constricted, so she undid the top button. She pressed her face to the window again, attempting in vain to see Main Street. A large, barrel-chested man hobbled along West Road, and as he got closer, she realized he was watching her with interest. She stood back hastily, leaving the faintest of imprints on the glass, then sat down, fiddling nervously with the lace at her wrists.

Five

The Letter

Manny lay waiting in Mr. Alderman's stable, both agitated and irritated. His shoulders ached, and he had a thumping headache. His stared at the farmer's ancient single-barrel shotgun slung over the door lintel. In other circumstances, Manny might have been more interested in handling the old relic, but now he put it from his thoughts. He'd not slept a wink, as uncertainty and questions had kept him awake all night. It all nagged at him—the Mormon association with his father's crime, the fear in his mam's voice, the extreme hostility of his brother, the secretiveness of Mr. Alderman's warning not to disclose his baptism yet, not to mention the possibility of hallucinations, and on top of all this, the unsettling thought that he was somehow repeating his father's choices. It left Manny confused, weary, and exhausted. And yet, the idea of turning his back on his spiritual conviction was unthinkable.

He brushed straw from his coat. It was pointless to knock at the farmhouse again, because he'd already tried. He must be patient. But patience was a quality he didn't possess in abundance this morning, so he thumped on the door anyway. Where was the housekeeper? Manny circled the farmhouse, tapping and pushing at each of the ground-floor windows in turn, just to make sure. But there was definitely no sign of either the housekeeper or Mr. Alderman.

The distant sound of cattle drifted across the valley, and mist slowly drew back from the farm, but Manny hardly noticed. He thought on how different it all might have been if his mam and Will had given him their support. He tried to imagine the circumstances of living here with Mr. Alderman and wondered how Hope would respond when he told her what his mam had let slip. It intrigued Manny to think his father had been so close to doing the very thing Manny had in fact done.

Having stayed awake all night thinking about the events of the previous day, he now craved rest. His eyes burned and his muscles ached. It was hard to think clearly. Tired as he was, he knew that if he fretted for too long he would lose grip on any sensible judgment. It was also possible that Hope might return with Mr. Alderman at any moment, and he wanted to feel composed for her arrival. Aware of the fact that he still hadn't asked for permission to marry her, Manny disliked the idea of being found asleep when Mr. Alderman returned.

When they still hadn't arrived by midday, Manny decided he couldn't stay where he was any longer. He must go back to Northwood. No doubt, he thought guiltily, Hope was already worried about why he'd been gone all this time.

He made straight for the bridle path. It would be better to travel over the moorland. That way he'd avoid meeting villagers who might ask awkward questions—like why he wasn't at work. Besides, over the moorland was the way Mr. Alderman always traveled, and perhaps they would meet.

The air on the moorland was cold, the hills damp beneath the mist. Manny's coat collar pressed against his neck, chafing as he walked. He tried to imagine himself herding sheep. He fancied he'd make a reasonable shepherd. The employment could tide them over until he found something more permanent. Since he was no longer obliged to work in a mill, he fancied he might try his hand at anything he pleased, so long as Hope could be supported. Though he had never expressed his dream of being a newspaper correspondent, why not try now? Mr. Alderman clearly felt well disposed toward the vocation, and with a fair commitment and steady effort Manny imagined he might do worse than to try. Hope could teach him the principles of grammar. It didn't hurt to dream—it made him feel dignified.

The mist was turning to rain. Bowing his head against the wind, he strode on a little faster. The footpath, littered with broken stone, wound steeply down, round an outcrop of rock, and led to the moorland road that would take him to Northwood.

He steadied himself and descended quickly. At the bottom, the path leveled out. It was now no longer possible to see the village.

Then, perhaps twenty paces ahead, and beneath the mist, he saw a body stretched out face down on the ground. It took a moment for Manny to grasp who it was. He stumbled forward, his heart crashing in his throat.

"Mr. Alderman!"

Manny grabbed the farmer by his coat and heaved him over. Blood and mud were smeared on his face. Grass had stuck to a gash on his forehead, a wound that ran from the bridge of his nose all the way up to his hairline. A thin trickle of blood had congealed in his hair. Mr. Alderman's eyes opened a little.

Manny shook him, trying to rouse him. "What happened?"

"I— attacked. Don't know . . . letter . . . concerning Hope." The old man's breathing was shallow, but his voice, though weak, sounded desperate. "In . . . my coat. Obadiah Thomas— Thomas—see it. Confide . . . no one else. Don't show Hope until . . . He's . . ." Mr. Alderman coughed and then closed his eyes. "Northwood."

Manny pulled Mr. Alderman up toward him. "No, you can't sleep—you can't just lie there. You have to get up."

Hope's guardian smiled weakly. "Look after— get through this . . . unite. Promise me." He took a breath and winced as if it caused him pain. "I've put money . . . for you, Manny. Want you . . . have. Vase . . . in the sitting room. Careful . . .

he'll be . . . dangerous." Mr. Alderman closed his eyes and shivered. "I'm cold."

"Get up. Come on, you've got to get up." Manny thought about trying to pull him back along the footpath. No, he couldn't do that. It might cause more injury.

He removed his coat and laid it across Mr. Alderman's body. Hesitating for a second, Manny wondered if it was safe to leave a person in such a condition. But there was no choice. If only . . . Gritting his teeth, he turned his back on the farmer and sprinted back toward Ormley.

Manny rounded the side of the farmhouse, breathing hard from the exertion of his running, and then collided with his brother.

"Hey, what . . ." Will began.

Manny stepped back, coughing, trying to regain his breath. "Mr. Alderman—he's out there . . . on the moors. He's been attacked. He must have been there all night. He's a terrible chill—he's soaked to the bone."

The news seemed not to have registered. Will was moving so slowly. He narrowed his eyes doubtfully. "You should be at work."

Sweat trickled down the side of Manny's face. Had Will not heard what was wrong—did he not care? Manny stared at his brother in disbelief, then turned and started back up the hill.

"Do you not want to know about your mam?" Will called after him. "She was crying all night for you. Didn't know where you'd gone—thought you'd left us. You know you could get punished for this."

Manny felt his face burning. "Are you going to help me or not?"

Will gave a frustrated look and ran to join him.

A short time later, they backed into Mr. Alderman's sitting room, his limp body sagging between them. Water dripped across the sitting room floor, and Manny wished the fire was not out and the room not so cold. They struggled over to the armchairs and eased the farmer into one of them. His lips were blue.

Manny's heart pounded. Gently he shook Mr. Alderman. He couldn't die. He couldn't.

Will stepped away, running his hands over his hair. "What happened to him, lad? How did this happen?"

Manny knew they didn't have time for discussion. "He needs warmth—he's cold as death. We need to get blankets."

"This is because of you, isn't it, lad? He were going to try and find Hope, weren't he?" Will was distraught. "What did I tell you? I told you no good would come of the Mormons. Look what it's done to your mam and me." He pointed at Mr. Alderman. "Look what it's done to him. Leave the Mormons be, before it makes more trouble."

Manny tried to keep his voice calm. "It's not just me that's making trouble."

"What do you mean by that?" Will asked as if he wanted to argue, but then he turned to leave the room. "Never mind."

Manny grasped Mr. Alderman's hands. They were cold, stiff. He couldn't die when he was supposed to be helping them. Manny remembered the letter.

Will's footsteps echoed away down the corridor. Manny reached inside Mr. Alderman's coat, his hands suddenly clammy. It felt wrong to be doing this, like he was stealing. The first pocket was empty. He touched another one, felt the crisp edge of an envelope. He pulled it out. He turned the letter over, transfixed, as the door swung open.

Will, blankets piled high to his face, walked across the room. Manny pulled the envelope close to his chest and dropped down to arrange the wood in the grate.

"Haven't you started that fire yet, lad?"

Manny shoved the envelope into his shirt and grabbed a log.

"I don't know, lad. I think you might be too late anyhow."

Mr. Alderman's head was back, his mouth open wide, his face gray.

Manny rose and bent to put his ear close to Mr. Alderman's mouth. There was still breath. As he straightened, the envelope slipped from under his shirt and landed at his feet.

Before Manny could move, his brother had bent down and seized it. "What's this, lad?" Will looked at the writing and tilted his head questioningly as he edged closer. "It's his, isn't it? Have you taken something as don't belong to you?"

Manny shifted his balance. "It's not for you, Will."

His brother didn't flinch. "Don't try that with me, lad. I know what you're doing. Me own brother . . . me own brother's a thief." He stepped forward and prodded Manny's chest with his finger. "You don't fool me. You might have tricked Mam and Hope and Mr. Alderman, but you won't deceive me. You need teaching a lesson for this."

Manny looked around the room in desperation and saw the china vase. It was right there, across the room, on the windowsill. He jumped forward, snatched the letter, and rushed toward the window. He felt Will's hand on his shoulder, gripping him tight. Manny pulled away, then lunged across the table, reaching out and grasping the vase. Books spilled onto the floor, and the table cracked.

Will shouted, "If you carry on like this, lad, I'll have you whipped." He had Manny pinned, held down against the table. "I will, lad. I promise. I'll make you pay."

There was the sound of loud knocking at the front door.

Manny's grip on the vase slackened, and he felt his brother prying it loose. Sunlight angled into the house through the window over their heads. It swept across Hope's portrait and then faded. Counsel Elder Armitage had given Manny after the baptism flashed into his mind. "Your life will get better," he'd said. "Don't give heed to the anger of those who do not understand. At the end of time, you will judge your life and feel the consequence of it. You see, you are being a leader—for your friends, for your village, for your family throughout the ages."

The sitting room door opened. It was Mr. Reeve. Obviously shocked at the scene of chaos, he hesitated just long enough for Manny to take advantage. Pushing Will away, he clenched the vase, then shouldered Mr. Reeve out of the way and stumbled from the room.

Manny thought he was vaguely aware of his mam standing at Mr. Alderman's garden gate, aghast at the scene of disorder emanating from the farmhouse. She raised her hand as if to call her son back. Manny slipped as he looked at her, smashing his ankle against a rock. But he ran on in spite of the pain, clutching the vase and the envelope tight to his chest. He ran blindly, ignoring the pain searing through his ankle, up and along his leg.

Into the open expanse of moorland he ran. It didn't matter where now. It mattered only that he got away—from Will and Mr. Reeve, from his horrified mam, and from the dying Mr. Alderman.

The ground in front of Manny suddenly dropped away into a ditch, and, too late to stop himself, he tripped and fell headlong. He lay winded, sprawled out on the dirt. Then, wiping peat from his mouth, he gathered up the vase and the letter and sprinted on before anyone might catch and apprehend him.

He kept running until he reached Shepherd's Well. Only then did he slow down and walk, his lungs burning. Shaken, he slumped down against the tree that overlooked the tarn below. Once he regained his breath, he briefly took stock of his hiding place, looking for a spot where he could keep out of sight.

The tarn was surrounded by huge outcrops of rock, and Manny climbed down them to get close to the water's edge. He sat down beside it, hugging the vase to his chest, then winced as he finally noticed the throbbing in his ankle. He doubted his brother had seen him run this way, and as a place to rest it was as good as anywhere, for now. He needed to gather his thoughts, he needed to be calm. Somehow, out of all of this madness, he needed to regain some control.

He looked in the vase. How much money had Mr. Alderman given them?

The money had been wrapped in oilskin. Manny opened the cloth and gasped. There were coins—a lot of them, perhaps fifty or more. And they were all sovereigns. Manny swallowed, overwhelmed at thought of the treasure before him, and then immediately felt guilty because the excitement seemed like greed, and the greed had made him forget both Hope and her guardian. But so much money. Clearly, Mr. Alderman wished them to succeed.

Manny picked up the envelope and turned it over, stroking the writing. He slid his finger under the flap, wrestling with the desire to read the letter. No. He mustn't. He must take it to the other man first, do what had been requested.

He scooped the coins back into the cloth, wrapping them carefully, and then shoved it all into his pocket. Mr. Alderman's motionless body had been so cold, so stiff, so lifeless. That gaping mouth . . .

Staring at the letter again, Manny cleared his mind and tried to think of something else. What had Elder Armitage told him about the Book of Mormon? "It was an ancient record," he'd said, "buried in the ground for centuries, and then given into the keeping of a farm boy at the hands on an angel." An angel. The elder's voice had become more urgent, more intent. "It's a record from God, carved on ancient plates—hidden, kept, and protected, translated by a prophet, for you. And it bids you to come and join us in Zion."

Manny pulled the Book of Mormon from his coat and turned it over thoughtfully. At the hands of an angel?

The china vase was cracked, and Manny threw it into the water. It floated briefly, tipped onto its side, and sank. The idea that Mr. Alderman might die sickened him, and he put the Book of Mormon back into his coat. He wished he did not suddenly feel so weary, so tired. He needed to think, needed to work out how he was to support Hope, how they were to go forward in the face of so much discouragement. Could it really be that his life had been turned upside down in the space of so little time? He wearily watched the mist creep across the tarn toward him, and then dragged himself underneath a protruding outcrop of rock.

The wind gusted against the tarn, and a smatter of rain unsettled the water. What if Will and Mr. Reeve got to Hope before he did? Manny needed to get back to her before them. He sat forward, biting his lip. On the other hand, they didn't know where she was. And they'd be telling the village about Mr. Alderman first. The pain in Manny's ankle was getting worse, and he loosened his bootlace to try to ease the throbbing. His head was heavy and his eyes stung. He must move on. But he had to rest first. He lay down, covering his face with his hands, and a deep and heavy weariness finally overpowered him.

Six

Betrayal

During the course of the afternoon, the sun had occasionally managed to filter through the Northwood smog. From time to time, Hope had squinted up at the sunlight, noting its slow turn from pallid yellow into the flaming amber fireball now burning behind the fading clouds. As the afternoon wore on, more and more shadows edged their way along the cobbles.

She had waited patiently all afternoon, here at this very spot in the parlor, not once leaving her place at the window. But now she felt an increasing desperation at the strangeness of Manny's disappearance. Yet it was she who had insisted on staying away, and she deeply regretted that she had waited so long before returning home. She was still fighting with conflicting loyalties—on the one hand, her wish to honor her father, and on the other, her desire to be a woman of independent will. The latter was not something the villagers would likely approve of, but lately Hope felt herself a reckless spirit and decided she didn't care for worrying over their good opinion anyway.

Why she had not already gone home she could not exactly explain, though she knew it would be a humiliating defeat now to trudge back alone. She turned away from the window in exasperation and then quickly turned back again. She couldn't bear not to be looking, and yet it added considerably to her frustration. The waiting had been awful; it was so helpless. She should never have stayed away.

After a time, she settled on finding her host again and on taking her mind off her torment. Hope smoothed the creases in her dress and was about to leave the room when, out of the corner of her eye, she saw a young man emerging out of the shadows and striding down West Road toward the house. It was Will. She watched as he slowed, gazing around as if unsure where to knock. Of course he had come to find her, and she knew at once that his coming meant something in Ormley was terribly wrong.

Turning from the window, she chastised her foolish decision to stay away from her father. It had been an act of sheer madness. Her lip trembled and tears pricked her eyes. Her hands shook, the palms suddenly clammy and cold.

When she ran from the room and flung open the front door, Will was still standing with his back to her, gazing around as if bemused. At the sound of Hope's cry he spun round to face her. They stood, each staring as if waiting for the other to speak the first word. Then, looking somehow reluctant, he hurried closer and stopped just in front of her, his eyes bloodshot and swollen.

"What—what is it?" She faltered.

He looked at her for what seemed an eternity. Then he muttered, "I'm sorry."

"What do you mean? What do you mean 'I'm sorry'?"

Will's face was white. He swallowed awkwardly. "I'm sorry. I wish it hadn't taken so long. I didn't know where to look for you. I've been looking . . . I've bad news." He stepped toward Hope and put his hand on her shoulder. She pulled away, confused by his manner.

Will rubbed his mouth, hesitating. Then, he reached out to take hold of her hand. "Hope, Mr. Alderman . . . your father—he's ill, very ill." Will looked past her as if embarrassed to meet her gaze. "He's in a really bad way. They think 'e could die before the end of the night! It were Manny what did it."

The news came with such speed that at first Hope could not comprehend the significance of it. She stood perfectly still. The words gradually came to have some meaning, and with them came the fear. Breathing quietly, she heard Will's insistent voice in her mind: "Hope, he's in a really bad way. 'E could die before daybreak!"

Without quite knowing what she was doing, she pushed Will away, shaking her head, slowly at first and then faster and faster, until the very street seemed to come loose from the ground. Everything was spinning, turning around her. She felt herself losing consciousness as darkness enveloped her.

When Hope came round, she found Sister Aitkin kneeling beside her. They were in the parlor of the lodging house. Hope's vision was blurred, and the back of her head felt sore. Will stood silently at the window, a motionless silhouette. But he must have been watching, because almost at once he crouched down beside her.

"What happened?" Hope whispered. For a moment she was genuinely unsure of where she was and of the grievous news she had just received. "Where am I?"

But as she saw Sister Aitkin, she remembered. "How long have I been like this?"

"Just a few moments, Hope love—that's what I would say. How do you feel?"

Hope's head ached, but her reply was simply to wince. She thought about what Will had said to her before she fainted. She struggled to prop herself up, angry at this cruel turn of fate, willing it not to be true.

"You must be mistaken, Will. It cannot be right. You are mistaken."

"I wish I were, Hope. But I've seen it all wi' me own eyes. I'm sorry."

She shook her head. It couldn't be true—it couldn't. "Where is Manny?" she demanded.

"I'm sorry, Hope. But you have to believe me, he's run away. Come with me, back to Ormley. Mam says you can stay wi' us, if you need to."

"How can this be Manny's fault? He would never do such a thing, you know it—we both know it."

Will's expression hardened. "It was his fault that your father had 'is accident, Hope. If he hadn't been so fixed on learning about the Mormons . . ." He paused and looked at Sister Aitkin. "Manny's turned against us all. He's lost his senses, run away. And to make things worse, he's stole some of your father's money, Hope." Will paused again and then said calmly, "Manny were wild, he stole it all from him. Can you not see he's gone mad? He's possessed. He's betrayed us all—me, Mam, your father, and now even you." He looked away, rubbing furiously at his forehead, then turned to face the window.

"He's lying, Sister Aitkin—that's what he's doing," Hope shouted. "He's lying. My father must have known we planned to . . ." She stopped, suddenly aware of just how much she didn't want Will knowing her affairs.

Sister Aitkin said nothing, but cradled Hope in her arms.

"I'm sorry, Hope," Will said meekly. "I wish it weren't true. I'd have come sooner but I had to get word t' the police." He seemed embarrassed by the confession of what he'd done, as if he held it as a matter of deep regret. "I came just as soon as I could. Mr. Reeve hi'self brought me here in his coach and four. He's insisted on helping. 'E reckons it's somehow his fault, that he should have paid Manny more wages. Mr. Reeve's waiting at the end of the street, to take us both back to the village."

Hope turned to Sister Aitkin. "Please come with me."

But Will stepped between them and said in a trembling voice, "Hope, leave this woman be. It's these cursed Mormons as have caused all this trouble." He glared as he said it, and, grasping Hope's hand, he pulled her up and led her out of the house.

⎯∞⎯

As Hope stepped out of the lodging house, she saw the coach. It blocked the end of West Road, glinting in the half light of the late afternoon. The horses strained at their bridles, foam dripping from their mouths as they shook their heads. Their coats shone with sweat. At first, Hope was surprised the mill owner himself had come for her, and then she felt terribly uncomfortable. He was not friendly with her father, and his sudden involvement in her affairs felt intrusive and unwelcome. It would be an unpleasant journey.

Mr. Reeve was watching her intently. He reached down to help her up, seeming stiff and abrupt. Resolved not to show her discomfort, she managed to smile, then took a deep breath and grasped his hand, conscious that Will stood behind her, waiting for her to get into the coach.

Women and children streamed into West Road. It was hard for Hope to see Sister Aitkin slowly stepping back into the shadows. Then she was gone.

An old man stood close to the horses. Hope had the distinct impression he had been the one to give away the whereabouts of Sister Aitkin's home. He smiled at Hope and touched his hat.

Mr. Reeve nodded curtly at him, closed the door, and sat down. "We thought we'd never find you,

Miss Alderman. We've been searching for ages. You can never be certain where these Mormons will hide, can you?"

Will leaned against the window, looking away from her. The carriage jolted forward and the horses trotted down Main Street, out onto the turnpike, past the workhouse on the edge of town, and then out into the darkening moorland. They traveled in silence, rushing deeper into the hills. The black dots of cattle in the distance blurred, and Hope closed her eyes and turned away from the window. Yesterday had been such freedom, such happiness as she was baptized, such happiness to imagine her wedding. But all of that was a distant memory. Now she was cold and alone, more than ever before.

Stones on the turnpike crunched and spat up from under the carriage wheels. Hope looked up and saw that Mr. Reeve was staring at her. In the dim light of the carriage, his face seemed almost skull like, his eyes sunk deep into gaunt sockets.

"My thoughts are with you, of course," he said. He smiled and then looked away. "But let me advise you to avoid mixing with the Mormons again. They'd love a charming girl like you."

The coach lurched as they rounded a bend, shook as they rode over the ruts in the highway. Hope struggled to keep herself from falling against Will. With a mixture of relief and dread she realized they were almost to Ormley. What kind of reception would there be for her?

Hope walked to the Shaws' kitchen window and turned her back on Lucy. She knew she ought to be more gracious, but she felt out of place here when she should be with her father. Will threw his coat onto the table and peered into a saucepan on the stove. He still seemed agitated.

"Please, we won't talk of Manny, my love," said Lucy. She leaned forward in her chair. "And I'm very sorry to hear the news of your father."

Hope turned to face her. "Is it really necessary that I'm here now? Would it not be better I came back later? I should really be with my father."

"We're expecting the police any moment," Will said quickly, avoiding her gaze. "You must be hungry," he mumbled, then bit into a piece of bread. "Can't I get you some'at to eat?"

Hope shook her head. It was completely inappropriate to have been brought here, but Mr. Reeve had insisted she be taken care of. She made straight for the front door. "No. Thank you. I'm going to see my father."

"But you'll need to speak with the police."

She started to protest about the lack of consideration when she was interrupted by a loud knock at the door.

Will looked at her. "That'll be them now." He squeezed past.

A large, pug-faced policeman stood sharply to attention on the doorstep, his ivory-white trousers contrasting a blue swallowtail coat. An imposing top hat was wedged firmly on his head. He peered in at them. "Shaws?"

"Aye, it is."

"I'm Constable Davidson." He looked over at Lucy and removed his hat. "May I come in?"

Lucy nodded. "I suppose you'd better had."

The policeman entered respectfully, surveying the room. "Sorry to hear the distressing news." When he saw Hope, he nodded knowingly. She wondered who else knew her business.

"It's a bad thing what's happened," he said gravely. "I believe the doctor 'as been with him?"

She nodded again. "And his housekeeper's keeping vigil with him now."

"To think how the young man acted with such callous disregard for you all. Mr. Reeve has fully informed me of the circumstances." Constable Davidson sat down and pulled out a notepad. "You understand, though, without evidence, me 'ands are bound? I'd not be able to secure a conviction without the proper evidence." He turned over a sheet of paper and looked up at Will. "So, what information can you give me that would prove the alleged crime?"

Will looked as if he was trying to gather his thoughts. "Me brother's disappeared. I saw him take a letter from Mr. Alderman. And then he took money and stowed it in a vase. You can see at the farm there were a fight." Will rolled up his sleeves and showed the grazes on his arms. "I don't know what else to say. You'll just have to trust me. I'm telling you the truth."

Hope wanted to be anywhere but in this house. She stood by the window, gripping the sill, trying to maintain her composure. Outside, a woman and two men were huddled in a group, talking. One of them pointed to the house, saw Hope, and stopped pointing.

She heard Lucy clear her throat as if struggling with something. "It's true, Constable Davidson. I believe my William is telling the truth. Mr. Reeve said how he saw Manny run from the farmhouse, carrying something under his arm."

Hope closed her eyes, willing herself not to cry. Not here, not in front of them. But she couldn't hold back all of the tears. She wiped at her cheek. What did Manny think he was doing?

Constable Davidson stared at her, but he addressed them all. "Delicate time for the village, this. Those Mormons are dangerous. And they're bigamists, illusionists, you know. But give 'em no heed and they'll pass us by soon enough."

Hope was caught off guard, her face suddenly hot. She turned sharply. "Bigamy?"

"Aye, miss. Marry as many as they like. I think they call it polygamy."

Lucy frowned, wringing her hands. Hope noticed Will smirking in the corner of the room. He saw her and had the grace to cover his mouth with his hand.

Hope drew back, turning her head so they wouldn't see her tears. Sister Aitkin hadn't told her anything about polygamy. The woman must know of it, but she'd said nothing. Nothing at all. Manny had fallen for trickery. Hope chastised herself for being such a headlong fool.

"Now then," the constable said, "a few more details if you don't mind, for the investigation.

Can you tell me what Manny was wearing, which direction he headed in—when you saw him last?"

"I can tell you where I reckon he went," Will said. "I reckon he'll have gone somewhere near Shepherd's Well."

"Aye, I know the place you mean, Master William. Used to walk to it when I was a boy. I'm from a village west of Northwood myself. It were a full day's walk . . ." He looked at his notes again. "Could you just give me a brief description of his clothes, his size, and so forth, if you wouldn't mind, please?"

Hope's face felt like it was on fire. "Manny's a bit like his brother—slim, dark-haired."

The force in her voice must have been obvious, because Will spun round to look at her, surprise written all over his face. He turned back to Constable Davidson and said, "I think he had his coat. He was wearing a shirt and dark trousers."

The kitchen was silent but for the pencil scratching the paper. The policeman finished and then stood, holding his hat under his arm. "I wonder, Master William, if you'd come with me later? I've to visit Mr. Reeve presently, but I'd like to inspect the tarn this evening."

"Aye, if you want."

"Two's safer than one, I always say. We've had reports of vagrancy. You can never be too careful." Constable Davidson strode to the door and looked back at Hope. "If there's anything else I can do, miss." His chest swelled as he inhaled, and his brass buttons strained to hold his coat together. "Just leave it to the law."

She nodded weakly. The front door clicked shut. But all she could think of was the idea of Mormon men marrying lots of women. The thought of her wedding made her sick. And now her father was paying for all of her foolishness. "I'm going to the farmhouse," she said. As she noticed Will reaching for his coat, she added, "I'll go on my own."

Seven

Alone, Together

I knew what it was to be at the center of a storm surrounding the Mormons. I'd experienced it myself in the late summer of 1837.

"I know what you are thinking, but your life will be better," Elder Fielding had said to me when I told him of Edward Reeve's displeasure. I hadn't known Elder Fielding for long, but I knew his extended family were British, and I felt he could understand the dilemma I faced. The idea of baptism was deeply appealing, and yet I found myself in an intolerable situation. I had been threatened with the loss of my job, and though initially curious, Lucy was fully against my interest in the Mormons as well. Elder Fielding had seemed grave, yet there was buoyancy in his voice. "What you are doing here in Ormley will roll out, down through the years, and be a great blessing in the end." He leaned closer. "Don't be put off by the anger of those who cannot understand, or by those who refuse to understand. Such treatment

has always been the lot of the faithful. What matters is your commitment to the things you know to be vital. No one else should live your life for you. When you want to feel close to God, that is a privilege you must come to privately. You do not need to rely on my faith—indeed, you cannot and must not. You have your own life to live, and with it, questions and answers you must find, answers you must own. For no one should take away your right to make a choice—no one can take your place at the end of time. You will answer for your own actions, for your own convictions, and not for mine. Not for Edward's or his wife's, or anyone else's. So you see, Isaac, what you may be is brave—a leader to your friends, for your village, and for your posterity through the ages."

I had looked at him, the face of earnestness, of invitation and possibility, and for a time I believed all would be well. My journey to the Mormons had begun by accident, or perhaps more accurately, by the hand of Providence.

I'd been standing, shoulders hunched against the cold, at the edge of the Liverpool docks, holding a sleepy Manny tightly in my arms, trying to shield him from the wind that whipped in off the sea. Lucy stood close beside me, also huddled against the wind, holding Will's chubby little hand. We watched the ships coming into harbor from various places around the world. In spite of the cold wind it was a day to be happy. We felt fortunate to have been able to take this rare excursion together, a rest day from the mill, an experience we'd never before had as a family. One could hardly call Liverpool docks a place of beauty, but there was most certainly something inspiring about seeing this port that led to the rest of the world. And so there we all were, enjoying this rare opportunity to spend time together, away from the village.

It was the heart of summer, and the port teemed with those who had disembarked and those awaiting departure. The air was filled with clamoring voices and the screech of gulls that wheeled overhead, the distant clanking and banging of horse and carriages and trains. There was the smell of the ocean and the smog from the town. It was hardly a tranquil outing. I sneaked a look at Lucy and wondered wryly at the irony of this being my family's first excursion. She smiled back at me. I knew then that she didn't care that we had only come to Liverpool. Time like this was as rare to us as seeing the rubies and riches of India itself.

I had lately been trusted with the oversight of Ormley Mill, and I knew Edward Reeve trusted me completely. We had come to be on good terms, and he'd been shocked to discover that in all the years of our marriage, Lucy and I had never been away from the village for even a single day. So when Edward was urgently required to travel to London on the same day that his wife, Mrs. Ellen Reeve, was due to arrive in Liverpool after visiting India, he requested that my family act as the welcome party. He'd smiled at me—his infectious, broad grin—and told me there was no one he trusted more wholeheartedly to bring his wife safely home than Lucy and me. Privately, I had begun to feel sure there might shortly be an increase in my responsibilities at the mill, and an increase in my wages—such was the esteem I felt Reeve held me in. So with excitement and gratitude, there we were—the four of us in Liverpool, happy to be together as we awaited the arrival of the Britannia *and Edward Reeve's wife.*

We'd been waiting for almost an hour when my attention was drawn to a ship, the Garrick, *gliding into dock. Some of the passengers leaned over the side, a few of them waving to the waiting crowds. The ship was very close. I watched in amusement as a balding, stocky man leaped from the landing boat and onto the jetty, without waiting for the boat to be tied. Here was a man for whom life bore meaning. I couldn't help but wonder at what his cause for so much good cheer could be. Though our paths were never to cross again, I later learned that this was Heber C. Kimball.*

I watched him carefully, wondering at what this enthused man thought of the great, looming buildings that overlook the docks, and it was then that I felt the first witness, a piercing light that reached inside of me and compelled me to smile. I noticed with some surprise that I had tears in my eyes. In that moment I could not have explained to anyone else why I felt so overcome, and yet I knew God was touching my soul. I felt certain I would learn the reason this man had leaped so eagerly ashore. Whatever it was that drove him on with such enthusiasm would one day be made known to me, and my life would be forever changed by it. I lost sight of him as the crowds swept him away.

Later, on the journey home, I fancied that both Lucy and Mrs. Reeve noticed a change had come over me, though they did not press me to speak of it. I could see that Lucy was kept from probing because of the fractiousness of our children, and I forbore from saying anything more. I might mention at this juncture that I had considered the question of religious affiliation a number of times, but felt disinclined toward the high churches and more interested in the chapels. I was not alone in this feeling; many of those who lived as Lucy and I did were, likewise, more inclined to nonconformity. Somehow it felt more pertinent to our lives. For a time I considered the primitive Methodists, but intention never came to be reality, and for the most part I stayed away. This was not to say I had no interest in such things. I considered that I had simply not found the right congregation for me. Lucy frequented the small Baptist chapel that lay on the highway exactly halfway between Ormley and Northwood. I acquiesced to attend from time to time, though I often joked that it was merely the halfway house and that at some point my journey must continue.

Weeks passed, and little more was said of the matter. Work at the mill became all-consuming, and the memory of the feeling began to lose some of its intensity. Then, one day, as I was passing through Northwood, I happened upon a man I'd noticed in the same landing boat as the balding, enthusiastic one. This other man was addressing a large crowd who had gathered to hear him speak. I lingered, and as he spoke of angels and prophets, of visions and revelation, I found I was again intensely moved. I was excited by the thought that God might once again have spoken as he had done so often in the days of Jesus and the Apostles, and I had no other desire but to stay where I was and listen. After the crowd moved away, I was the only one left, so I ventured to speak with the man who had preached.

Manny woke suddenly. He'd been in Liverpool, by the docks, a child in his father's arms. He stared into the night, somewhere between wakefulness and sleep. Then the moonlight slipped back across the surface of the tarn, and he remembered where he was. Somewhere in the distance, a dog barked. Manny's muscles stiffened as he sat up and looked around. It was dark—it was late. He was a fool. He'd slept far too long. How could he have allowed himself to do such a thing? And yet the dream had seemed so important. But Hope would be beside herself, and anything might happen if Will had found her.

There was no more time to be lost. Manny wondered how he would tell Hope about Mr. Alderman, the turn of their fortunes, and the hostility increasing toward them.

Manny saw the letter lying at his side and grabbed it. A breeze gusted across the tarn, tugging at the surface of the water. Tiny waves rolled in toward him, and the moon's reflection slipped back again. He checked for the money bag and stood up. He had to get to Northwood quickly now. He ran his fingers through his hair, trying to work out what to do. What was the name of the man Mr. Alderman had said to him? Obadiah Thomas? Manny had never heard of the man before. He wondered about opening the letter and then stopped himself. It didn't seem right.

Kneeling by the edge of the water, he cupped his hands and splashed his face, alert to the darkness. Something moved on the other side of the tarn—it sounded like boots scraping on rock. In the darkness, a pebble clipped the granite. It rolled over another rock and then dropped into the tarn.

The air was quiet but for the lap of water at Manny's feet, then something that sounded like a sneeze, scuffling, and a bleat.

He breathed out in relief and shook his head, waving his arms. "Go on, get, yah . . ."

The sheep skittered away, scattering more stones as it fled. Manny laughed at himself, but his hands still shook, and he felt the goosebumps on his arms rubbing against his sleeves. He scooped another handful of water, trying to put the fear from his mind. He drank slowly and then smiled that he had let himself be scared by an animal. But thoughts of the moorland assault on Mr. Alderman still nagged at him. Manny quickly splashed water on his face again and stood. His nerves were getting the better of him. He needed to get going.

The tarn was silent once more; there was just the soft whistle of wind in the trees. He tried to stave off images of the apparition he thought he'd seen near the farmhouse the night before. The wind whipped against his face, and he heard the sound of more sheep, calling out from the moorland.

Then there was another sound—where the sheep had previously been. And Manny waved his arms. "Go on—"

There was someone there—the figure he'd seen in the woods, the face half hidden behind the brim of the hat, just like it had been before, the shadow stretching out across the tarn, fluttering like a blackened flag. Then the person moved swiftly back and out of sight.

Manny could hear nothing but the thumping of his heart. His shout had lodged in his throat, and he felt as if his entire body was paralyzed. Then, mercifully, he could move again. He scrambled back from the edge of the water and ran to the outcrop of rocks. He tried to climb quickly away, but his feet slipped and he slid back, scraping his shins and hands.

He tried to hear where the person was, but there was no sound. He got slowly to his feet and tried again to climb, this time a little more carefully. He hauled himself up, and at the brow of the rock he hid behind a boulder, holding his breath. There— the sound of footsteps, the stranger getting closer. Then silence. Cloud passed over the moon and the moorland became dark.

Manny heard voices. Turning in the direction of the sound, he saw the dull yellow light of a lantern dipping and swinging, as whoever was holding it came slowly nearer. He slithered back, moving quietly, keeping low to the ground. The stranger also seemed to have noticed that someone else was approaching, because the tarn remained in complete silence.

Manny saw two men gazing down at the tarn, the lantern light illuminating the area immediately around them. He tried to make out who they were, and then heard the familiar sound of Will scuffing his clogs. The light moved. The other man was a police constable.

Manny heard a noise behind him, so quiet he almost missed it. But he knew what it was. The stranger was no figment of his imagination. He felt a presence behind him, creeping slowly through the bracken. Twisting round, he tried to locate movement, but it was too dark to see anything. He thought about running, of giving himself up. But Will had kept to his threat. There would be little sympathy. There was no knowing what lies he might have spun. Manny bit his lip and stayed where he was.

The lantern light moved. The sound of feet and falling shale and stone revealed that the searchers were now investigating the place where he had been hiding. Any moment now they would see him. How could they not detect his presence? They came closer.

Will stood inches from Manny's hand. Only the darkness hid him, but if the lantern light was moved, as it surely must be, it would all be over. It seemed an age before Will moved on, moving down to the spot where Manny had been washing only minutes before. He stood there at the edge of the tarn, his hands shoved deep into his pockets. He crouched by the water's edge and then rose quickly, climbing back up to the waiting policeman.

"I reckon he'll be in Northwood by now, anyway."
Manny's brother said before disappearing into the
darkness.

The constable held up the lantern again and
gazed round at the tarn. Manny could see his great,
hulking face peering down, scanning the shadows.
Then, he too turned and walked away.

As the sound of their footsteps faded, Manny
was unsure whether to feel glad for their departure.
The moorland descended into silence again, and
he watched the lantern light fade.

There came a sound like a whisper, low
and urgent. His mind filled with a vision of Mr.
Alderman's battered face. Manny kept his face low
and slid back from the sound, his hands slipping
in the peat as he moved away. The ground was
cold, soaked from the rain, and muddy. He could
run or he could hide, but he felt caught in between.
The damp chill of the moorland was creeping into
his hands and knees and feet. He lifted his head
then raised himself slowly. There was a noise like
somebody whispering again, and Manny stood up
and ran.

He'd forgotten how close he was to the edge of
the quarry. The ground dropped away sharply, and
he grabbed to stop himself falling, realizing too late
what had happened. The drop was steep, and his
body jarred as he hit the slope, his leg snagging in
a gorse bush. He tried to pull himself round but he
couldn't, and his weight ripped him free. Then he
was rolling faster and faster until finally he landed
awkwardly at the bottom of the quarry, hitting his
head on a rock. He blacked out.

Eight

Help

Hope pulled the blanket closer to her father's chin, trying to keep him warm. It was strange to see him like this—so weak, so vulnerable, so near to death. His skin was now almost translucent. With no small surprise she realized how much she loved him, and how sorry she felt that she had been unable to feel closer to him.

He was a kind man. He had always been so decent, so long-suffering. Never a harsh word had she heard him utter. She loved him in spite of his reticent manner and felt a deep sense of gratitude for the way in which he had taken her in as an orphan. Whatever recent resentment she might have nursed because he would not speak further of the circumstances of the adoption was transcended by the alarmingly close proximity of death. An overwhelming sense of goodwill and forgiveness was all she could feel for this gentle man who had taken her in, this man who had persevered in caring for her in spite of his own wife passing away when Hope was merely eight. Death, she knew, was a frequent caller in these parts. Short lives were simply a fact. But even so, Hope was struck for the first time by how curious a fact the oncoming of death actually was, how its looming cut through the chaff of everyday trivialities and forcibly showed where the wheat might have been harvested.

She took possession of her wandering thoughts and tried to control her doubts. Her father was yet alive; there was no cause for giving him up to the grave. Will had exaggerated the danger her father's life was in. There was no reason to believe he must die.

She'd lit a small fire in the grate and had kept it burning brightly all evening, but the fireplace was small, and since the bedroom had always been drafty, the heat of the flames had only ever served to take the chill out of the air. Right on cue the wind picked up as it routinely did, whining at the windowpanes. The candles sputtered on the sill, threatening to go out. The flames' reflection ebbed and then rose on the porcelain pitcher next to the candles. The pitcher was still full, as no request for water had been made yet. Just as there had been no requests for water, or for that matter anything else, neither had there been any recognition of Hope from her father. Instead, he had simply lain perfectly still, occasionally staring with glassy eyes at the ceiling. But there had been no speech, and although he had opened his eyes earlier, he had not stirred since.

Sweat speckled his brow and he let out a slight moan. Hope picked up a wet cloth from the washstand. She squeezed the cloth tightly over the basin, angry and upset at his condition and blaming herself for it, then shook the water from her hand and dabbed gently at her father's brow, trying not to apply too much pressure to the most bruised areas of his face. His mouth twitched as if the application hurt him, and she thought for a moment that he might speak, but he didn't. She dropped the cloth back onto the stand and sat down, heart heavy with guilt. He looked terrible.

Water dribbled from the stand and then dripped slowly onto the floorboards. Hope picked up the cloth again, gripped it in both hands, and pressed it to her forehead, trying to soothe the aching throb that burned her brow.

When the bedclothes moved, she turned quickly. Her father's eyes were open, and he was staring at her.

"Hope," he mumbled. He tried to sit up. "Where's Manny?"

"Keep still, Father."

"A drink, I'd be grateful if you could . . ." He closed his eyes. She hastened to retrieve the pitcher of water and heard him mumble something else. Turning instinctively to look at him, she tried to grasp what he had said. But apparently he knew she had not caught his message the first time and repeated, "There's a new Bible on my desk. Could you bring it?"

Hope's hand shook as she poured water from the pitcher. What did he mean? For what purpose could he want the Bible? Was she to read it to him? She pressed the cup to his lips but he didn't respond, so she set it on the floor by the bed. Kneeling by his side, she clasped his hand. "I'm sorry, Father. I'm so sorry for causing all this trouble."

He didn't answer. She pushed herself up, walked over to the window, and picked up one of the candles. Shielding the flame with her hand, she left the room and descended the darkened stairs. In the sitting room, her father's books lay scattered across the table, and she reached for the black Bible at the top of the pile.

Still heavy hearted, and now slightly confused about the meaning of this request, she returned to her father, the book tucked firmly under her arm. In the bedroom, she placed the candle on the dresser and thumbed through the pages. The paper smelled new, and she felt certain she'd not seen this particular Bible before. Then, holding it gingerly with both hands, she sat down next to the bed and began to read. And as she read the memory of her baptism and the missionary and Sister Aitkin all came crashing back.

She wondered how she could have allowed herself to fall for a lie. It was all too good to be true—the feelings, the hope, the sense of an angelic presence. She could see now that it was all in vain. Her life was destined to be filled with disappointment. Why did she have to be so unfortunate? Tears welled up and she covered her face with her hands. The Bible slipped from her lap and slapped the floor at her feet. It had been such a peaceful feeling to step out of the river after the baptism. If only it had really been angels she'd felt. But then how could it have been? If Mormons really were polygamists and illusionists, as Mr. Reeve and Constable Davidson had suggested, how could she have felt so happy being with them? Surely she would not be expected to share a husband, would she? If she and Manny got married that would mean . . . Hope shuddered and leaned down, grasped the Bible again, and smoothed out the creased pages. There was evidence of this type of marriage in this very book. She thought about taking it back downstairs.

"Hope, you must learn to trust your spirit." It was her father. She seized his hand.

He was staring at the ceiling again, but this time there was a tinge of red in his cheeks. "You can't see it yet, my love, but you have been favored. And God is watching over you."

"But if I'm wrong . . ."

Her father winced as he pulled himself up, gripping her hand. "No. God is in your dreams. God is in your future. The letter—read the letter."

This was the first Hope had heard of any such thing, and the information stopped her in her tracks. "Father, what do you mean? What letter?"

He closed his eyes once more but smiled peacefully. "Your father's an honest man." He said no more.

The Bible was open on her lap. She glanced down at a verse that had been underlined and gasped. Putting her finger on the paper, she traced the words. They seemed to rise from the page, and she whispered them under her breath—"Cast not away therefore your confidence, which hath great recompence of reward."

The significance of the verse dawned on Hope, and her mood lightened a little. She closed the book and opened the cover. There was writing scrawled on the title page, but the ink was blotchy and she had to hold it closer to make out the words. *A gift for a gift.*

She put the Bible down and stared out of the window. What did that mean?

There were brisk footsteps on the stairs. Hope closed the book, her thumb marking the verse she had just discovered.

The bedroom door opened, and the housekeeper peered in. "Hello, Miss Alderman. Sorry to have taken so long. I had to find someone to take your father's mail to Northwood." Then, softening a little, she asked, "How is he?"

"He's been talking a little. He seems delirious, though."

The housekeeper glanced down at the Bible. "And are you all right?" She stepped in. "I'm sorry, but I've a message from Lucy Shaw. She's asking if you'd mind letting them know about how Mr. Alderman's faring. I think she wants to give you a meal."

The housekeeper seemed embarrassed to be bringing such a request at this late hour, but while Hope was wary of traveling after dark she was not afraid to do so—even in the alarming circumstances that had left her father in such a condition. Ormley had always been such a peaceful place. It would be safe enough. And in spite of Lucy's unpredictability,

Hope understood how distressed she must be by all that had happened. Since Mr. Alderman was now showing some small signs of recovery, Hope thought it compassionate to tell her this. It wouldn't take her long if she walked quickly.

Hugging the Bible to her chest, Hope leaned over and kissed her father good night, then tiptoed from the room.

∞

The branches of the ash and oak trees drooped like arms in the darkness, hanging across the bridle path and obscuring the moonlight. Hope lingered in the quiet and listened to the bubble of the river, somehow comforted by this blanket of darkness and rejuvenated by being out of the farmhouse.

Standing by the bridge over the Orm, she remembered this was where Manny claimed to have seen his vision. She closed her eyes and leaned against the stone wall, clutching her Bible. Bats skittered above her, making her skin prickle. The village itself seemed to be asleep. There was no movement on the highway, no sound of people talking. It was so quiet.

It was one of the strange aspects of the Ormley folk—they tended to shun the usual community behaviors. There was little outside socializing. The village might have been accurately identified as a melancholy place. It was hardly surprising Manny was so keen to leave it. Anyone unfamiliar with the village might walk through it at any given time of the day and see only one or two people, but they would not find them talkative. It was as though they had all adopted the manners of Mr. Reeve, who generally kept himself shut away in his house, his mill, or his carriage.

Now, as usual, the village was still. Hope listened to the river tumbling past the mill and thought she could just make out the creak of the water wheel as it rocked back and forth in the surge. She stood for a while, enjoying the peace, reviving in the quietness. Then, turning her thoughts to the duty that lay ahead, she braced herself for supper.

In fact, the meal passed uneventfully—Lucy was courteous, and Will was out. As soon as Hope could reasonably excuse herself, she left, hurrying back along the highway toward the bridge. Lucy had been embarrassed that Hope would be unescorted. Will was nowhere to be found, having gone out on the moors with the police. Here the conversation had become a little stifled. But Hope had assured Lucy that she need not concern herself with arranging escorts and that she could certainly walk home alone in the dark. She had nothing to fear. The truth was, Hope was too distracted to care about the dangers. Besides, the thought of waiting for Will to return just so she might be escorted back to the farm by him was a good reason to leave early.

When she reached the bridge, she paused to regain the feeling of revival. As she made to move on, a noise stopped her. Someone had pushed open the mill gates and was crossing the courtyard. Whoever it was kept looking back. Then the figure passed into the moonlight. It was Will.

Hope might not have thought anything of it, had he not seemed so concerned about being seen. Compelled to follow, she crept after him. He'd disappeared through the arched entrance to the inner mill yard. She stood at the gates and then pushed them open. The hinges squeaked. But the mill was silent and she entered the courtyard.

Her boots clipped against the uneven flagstone. She passed into the darkness of the alley and stopped. Just ahead of her, light spilled from an open door. Stepping closer, she overheard Will's voice. He sounded excited and urgent.

"I found it at the tarn. Manny had it when he left the farmhouse. Said it were for Hope. It's Mr. Alderman's own handwriting . . . I can't read it."

"Show it to me."

That was Mr. Reeve. Hope held her breath and tiptoed closer. He sounded angry, but it was the kind of snappiness that came of fear. There was the sound of paper rustling, tearing. She knew Will had never taken to reading as Manny had. It was a sore subject for Will, a fact he bitterly resented.

She wondered why he hadn't brought her whatever it was he had discovered. There was silence for a few moments, then Reeve's voice. "You must see to it that Hope doesn't know about this letter, William."

Hope's surprise at hearing herself the subject of the conversation almost made her miss the change in Mr. Reeve's voice. His tone was now more paternal than angry. She took it to mean, however, that he was not reassured by what he had found, only glad he had found it. "It would only cause more trouble for your family if Hope and your brother should know what was in here."

"Why? What does it say?"

"Never mind that now."

"But . . ." For the first time, Will actually sounded unsure.

"Where is Constable Davidson?" Mr. Reeve asked.

"He's fetched another officer to help him do a search on the moors."

"Good. Then I suggest that I hold on to this letter for the time being, William. I think perhaps I'll take advice on it in the morning. Meanwhile, don't mention it to anyone. Let the police get on with the business of arresting your brother. It's no more than he deserves."

The door opened a little wider, and for a horrible moment Hope thought they would catch her. She stepped back and tripped but managed to stay upright. She quickly gathered her skirt, then ran and hid in the shadows.

Will and Mr. Reeve stepped outside and peered into the darkness as if checking to be sure they were alone. Hope tried to control her breathing. Her heartbeat seemed to thud all around the alleyway. But shortly the two men disappeared back into the office and shut the door.

She stood, feeling weak and shaken. Why had Will not told her about the letter when he'd known it was for her? Was this the letter her father had referred to? What did Mr. Reeve mean about trouble? Why the strained voice, the secretiveness?

Hope reproached herself for having been so quick to lose faith in Manny's good sense. It was Mr. Reeve and Will who were hiding something. They were plotting something against her. At least Reeve certainly sounded as though he was. She must find a chance to speak with Will. He wasn't so unreasonable as to go along with this, was he? Reeve was the man not to be trusted, not Manny.

She counted to three and then ran. She didn't stop running until she reached home.

$\mathcal{N}$ine

The Man from the Past

Orange light flickered, pulsing on the walls of a small stone room. Manny smelled smoke. Something heavy was draped over him. For a moment he thought he was in bed, at home—that he might be late for work. Then he felt a sharp throb of pain at the back of his head and remembered he was a runaway. He'd fallen. He pulled himself up. Something wasn't right. It was dark, still night. But the tarn was gone and so was the quarry.

With a shock, he realized he was lying on a narrow straw mattress and that the weight on his body was a thick wool blanket. There was another wave of smoke; the pulsing orange light came from a wood fire. Manny was comforted by the warmth in the room. Someone had taken pity on him. Then his headache worsened and he lay back.

Shadows jumped against the uneven stone walls, and wood smoke drifted over him, stinging his eyes. Hearing someone snoring softly, he turned to look at his benefactor. By the half light of the fire, he could make out a man, asleep, slumped in a chair in the corner of the room. With his head down and his chin resting against his chest, the man's long black hair obscured his face, He was broad, and his rolled-up sleeves revealed muscular arms. There was a gold ring in one of his ears, and a scarf around his neck. On the back of his chair was a broad-brimmed hat.

Manny gasped, wondering if he was losing his mind. The thought lodged in his head in spite of his effort to reject it, and he started to fret, his whole body prickling and hot in his panic. The back of his head still hurt and he felt paralyzed, unable to escape from this confusion. Perhaps it was all just a dream—a dream that seemed very real, a nightmare from which he would eventually wake up. He forced himself to turn over and realized his back was slimy with sweat. At last he managed to sit up, his head swimming. He felt as though he might be sick. And suddenly he knew he could not be dreaming.

Where was his money, the letter? He checked his pockets. They were empty. The man must have robbed him. No, that didn't make sense. If he'd done that, why would he have brought him back here?

Manny's mouth was dry. He wanted to move, but didn't. Then he felt foolish. He couldn't just sit on the bed and do nothing. The man hadn't hurt him—he'd been following him, and now he had taken care of him. Manny turned the quilt back slowly. A breeze swept under the door, causing the ashes of the fire to glow, and he realized where he was. This was the shepherd hut Mr. Alderman had told him about.

Manny could see his boots set carefully by the fire. He eased himself out of the bed and padded across the floor to get them. How long had he been asleep? The money bag was beside the man's chair. He crept toward it. Now that he was close to the man, he could see a deep scar running from the corner of the man's eye down to his chin, the skin around his cheek strangely hollowed and pocked. There was something oddly familiar about the man's face, but Manny couldn't think what it was.

How could he creep away like this? It suddenly seemed ungrateful to leave. He wasn't sure what to do. The man had clearly been looking out for him, and yet Hope was still unaware of all that had happened, and there was the letter that must be delivered. His hands went back to his pockets. The letter—where was it? He held his breath as he searched his trousers. His heart was pounding now, and he stared wildly around the darkened room, trying to see where the letter might be. The money bag. Perhaps it was in there. He mustn't check here, though, as it was sure to make a noise.

He picked up the bag and tiptoed to the door. Gripping the handle, he pressed down on the latch. The door creaked as he pushed it open. Behind him, Manny heard the man struggle up from his chair, then call, "Ephraim, wait!"

In the moonlight, Manny saw the silhouettes of two men creeping along the brow of the hill, not more than a few hundred yards away. The outline of men's tall hats and swallowtail coats meant only one thing: constables. Manny couldn't run as he'd surely be seen; he couldn't stay as he'd surely be found.

He pushed the door shut and leaned against it, trembling. "It's the constables—they must reckon I'm guilty of theft," he confided despite himself. "They'll look in here." Then a thought occurred to him and he turned to the man. "How did you know my name?"

The man stared back at him. "I'm a friend. I knew you when you were young." He pushed Manny away and opened the door, just enough to see out, then closed it. "And I sent Elder Armitage."

"You did what?"

But the stranger was bolting the door now. "You needed help."

"I needed . . . what do you mean?"

"If the police find me here they'll arrest me for vagrancy." The man looked round the room desperately, as if thinking quickly. "I need to hide," he said. Then, "Have you got the letter?"

Manny stared at him. "Are you Obadiah Thomas?"

The man shook his head, looking impatient. He held out his hand. "The letter."

But Manny knew without looking that he no longer had it. He had an awful feeling the letter had been lost at the tarn, but to show good faith he turned his pockets out and then peered into the bag. "I had it, at the tarn. But . . ."

"You've lost it?" For the first time, the man sounded alarmed.

"You scared me. I ran. I thought—" Then Manny realized something. "You know Mr. Alderman?"

The man nodded and grabbed Manny's arm. "Listen to me. That letter concerns us both, lad. It's a matter of utmost importance that it doesn't find its way to the wrong hands before . . ." He broke off from what he was saying to listen for the police. "We haven't got time."

Manny's headache had worsened, and he felt lightheaded. He was terribly thirsty. And now everything was converging on him at a furious pace with no obvious solution.

"Mr. Alderman's had an accident," Manny said. "I think he's close to death!"

By the look on the man's face this news was a shock. "Then we must try to prove the truth all the harder," he said. "Hide under the bed." The man was pulling Manny across the room and spoke rapidly now. "Mr. Alderman is a good man, as your father was."

Manny resisted the man's grip, completely thrown by this new revelation.

"Use this sackcloth," the man said. He pushed Manny to the ground and gestured for him to crawl under the bed. "It's dark in here. It might just work. If I can just get you some time . . ."

But Manny wasn't listening to the instructions and reached out, trying to make the man stop. "You knew my father?"

"Aye, he saved my life."

"He saved your life?"

"Aye, and I know he wasn't guilty of murder, or manslaughter, or whatever Edward Reeve accused him of. I'll try to divert the police long enough for you to escape."

"But . . ."

"Look, lad, if you don't help me, they'll have us both."

Manny's mind was spinning. There was so much he wanted to ask, and so little time. "Who are you?"

The man hesitated. "Listen. I've made mistakes, done things I shouldn't have. But I know you're innocent, I know what it is you want, and I want to help you. But you must find that letter. It has proof . . ."

There was the sound of lowered voices outside. The man began to whisper rapidly.

". . . that Hope is my daughter. There's bread and meat behind the chair. But get away as soon as I've distracted them, and find the letter, or we're all done for. I'll never be able to pay your father back for what he did, but maybe this'll help."

"Hope's your daughter? But . . . we thought . . ."

There was a loud knock, and the latch rattled as someone tried to open the door. A voice from outside called, "Police! Open in the name of the law."

The man picked up the money bag. "If Edward Reeve knows I'm back and gets wind that the letter has proof," he whispered, "he'll do everything he can to destroy it, and my credibility. Please, you must help me."

One of the policemen ordered the door to be opened again and called Manny's name, telling him to come out quietly. There was silence for a moment. The man looked at the door, as if readying himself for what he was about to do.

"Why would Reeve destroy the letter?" Manny whispered.

"Your father was a good man. He wasn't guilty. Edward was. He's hiding the truth about the deaths. His folly killed his wife, and then he made me leave the village. Listen, I met with George Alderman yesterday, shortly after you did. He said he was going to Northwood and that he would write a letter bequeathing fifty pounds to you and Hope, and would provide written testimony of who I am. He gave me someone else's name—Obadiah Thomas. He's a solicitor in Northwood. If you do fail to find the letter, he might be able to help."

"But I don't even know your name."

The man clutched the bag and made for the door. "It's John."

Manny pulled himself back under the bed, dragging the sackcloth in with him. He listened as the man drew back the bolt, flung open the door, and sprinted out. For a moment there was shouting, struggling, and then quiet.

⚬⚭⚬

I'd been invited into Mr. Reeve's very lovely home, and had been standing looking—a little wistfully, it has to be said—at a new pianoforte that had been lately bought in London and transported all the way to Ormley. I knew Edward Reeve was fond of playing music and that he frequently entertained guests from the city.

To my surprise, since I'd become Mr. Reeve's foreman he'd taken me under his wing and regularly asked Lucy and me to dine with him. We were, of course, flattered by these invitations. Edward Reeve was in this respect quite unlike his peers. He had also begun paying me such a wage that Lucy and I were quite taken aback. The one thing he seemed not to lack was generosity.

The room in which I had stood was large, with a polished wooden floor. A vast window enabled any and all who found themselves in the room to look out over the heather-covered moors. A silvery mist hung over the horizon, somewhat dulling the prospect. But knowing Ormley as I did, and knowing the window faced west, I fancied that the view in the evenings must have been extraordinary. With my own little family cooped up in such a humble home, a sudden rush of jealousy took hold of me, so much so that I couldn't feel at peace. Still, I reasoned I had a good wage and a generous employer—I was well enough off.

I'd found myself thoroughly unprepared for Mr. Reeve's reaction to my interest in Mormonism. Perhaps I ought not to have been. Naïvely, I thought that on account of our otherwise good rapport and his cheery nature, he would respond with interest at the very least, if not with the same enthusiasm I had felt. And indeed initially he had; he'd been warm and gracious, though a little busy, and I had spoken of it only briefly with him. I'd also mentioned the subject of my spiritual feelings to one other young couple—Edward Reeve's younger brother John and his wife, whom I had the pleasure of knowing on account of their having recently arrived in the village at the invitation of Mr. Reeve. It was, in fact, the new Reeves who were at first most interested in learning more of the Mormons, and the four of us had invited the elders into our home to tell us about the Restoration. George Alderman had subsequently joined our meetings. The message the elders brought was music to all of us. The idea that the heavens had been parted, that God himself had appeared to a young man in our times, just as angels had appeared in the days of the apostles, was thrilling, and we became convinced that what we had been told was the truth.

For the first time I was able to imagine a meaningful future for my family, and I longed to meet this Joseph Smith of whom I had been told. I knew then that I could help to establish a branch of the Church in Ormley. I vividly remember Lucy's countenance—the light in her face, eyes brimming with tears of joy that first night the elders visited with us. We hardly wished them to leave, and we could not contain our excitement at the world their teachings opened to us. Indeed, we remained awake for the whole of the night discussing what was to be done. I was committed to the idea of persuading Edward Reeve to listen too; I thought he would have been glad to hear what we had learned.

I was encouraged at first that he was kindly disposed to reading a copy of the Book of Mormon. He seemed genuinely touched that I would think of him, and I could see that the effect on him was one of light, as it had been with the rest of us. Thus I was astonished at the reaction I received shortly after

Reeve's return from a trip to London. It was late in the evening, and he was alone in his library. On his desk lay a copy of the Book of Mormon. I no longer saw in his face a cheery, gracious nature, but rather a strange darkness. He was curt, utterly without the capacity to receive me with the grace he had so obviously possessed before. He was distant and distracted. I wished there was something I might do to cheer him. I left him sitting in the darkness of his library, and with a feeling of deep regret, went straight home. Yet I said nothing to Lucy in respect of the conversation, hoping Mr. Reeve's melancholy would pass and that all good relations would be soon restored.

Ten

Another Leaving

Hope plucked at the lace she was making and then held it up to the light, trying to look intent on her work. She must maintain her composure and not give away her concern about what she had overheard at the mill. Will had been with her for almost an hour, moody and quietly watchful.

Out of the corner of her eye, she could see him, slouched on his chair in the corner of the room. She wondered what he was thinking—whether he had regrets about going to Reeve. She considered what he might say if he knew what she had heard, and how far Will would go in making out that Manny was a thief. In the light of her discovery, it now seemed utterly preposterous that Manny could ever have been thought a lawbreaker. He'd rather lose his right arm than shame his family in that way. Why he had run away was not a question she could answer, but she suspected it had something to do with Will.

She thought carefully. Her father had known of a letter; by all accounts he'd been assaulted on the moors. And now, as well as a missing letter, there was a Bible with a mysterious cryptic message. Hope glanced over at Will. Surely he could mean her no harm. Surely if she simply asked him to account for what had taken place he would respect her enough to acknowledge his actions. His heart was not so cold that he would turn his brother over to the police without proper cause. In his defense, Will had sounded unsure when Reeve demanded to keep the letter. Surely Will would welcome her help.

The lace hung from her trembling fingers like a cobweb. She put the lacework down quickly so as not to draw attention to her nerves, and then urged herself out of her agonizing and smoothed out the creases in the lace with a decisive stroke of her hand. She picked up her black Bible and opened it, rocking gently in her chair. The silence was broken only by the sound of the housekeeper's steady footsteps crossing the bedroom above, and the clock on the mantelpiece chiming ten. At the sound of the chiming Will had looked up, first at the clock and then at Hope. Her heartbeat quickened and her hands shook again. She turned another page. He must not suspect she was afraid. It was late, and he must already have wondered why she had not retired for the night.

She watched him leaning over her father's reading table, shuffling some of the books. He picked up the copy of *Paradise Lost*, opened it, and held the pages to the light, squinting at the print.

Then he peered at Hope over the top of the book and suddenly spoke. "I reckon I miss a lot with not taking to this." He was attempting to smile and almost looked humble.

"I'm sure you could learn, Will—you're very determined, when you put your mind to it." She couldn't resist adding, "And you'd find it helpful in so many ways."

At first there was no response, and then he looked down. "Hope, I'm sorry about what's happened to your father."

She nodded but didn't speak. Will was clearly trying to make up for his harshness. She knew he was shy beneath his bravado—sensitive like his brother. It was a pity he couldn't acknowledge his faults more easily. They might have been good friends. Perhaps there might be an opportunity to challenge him over what she'd heard at the mill.

Will smiled sheepishly and then his face reddened, as if he were embarrassed to be so open about his feelings. He tossed the book back onto the table and stood up. "Ah, well, I need to go. I've to oversee the weavers in the morning. And I'll bet you're half dead wi' lack of sleep anyhow. Tell us if there's anything I can do."

He waited for Hope to respond, and when she didn't he nodded toward the broken table. "I'll send a man up to fix it for you in the morning." He looked as though he was trying to make peace. He smiled at her again, flushing slightly, and then turned to leave. "Like I said if there's anything you need . . ."

"Will, there is one thing."

He stopped in the doorway, and when he turned back he looked genuinely surprised, even flattered. "Aye, what is it?"

Hope wondered about the wisdom of challenging him now about what she had overheard, knew it was a risk, but she committed herself. "Why didn't you tell me about that letter?"

If Will was taken aback he barely showed it. There was only the slightest glimmer of recognition. Then he stared at her impassively. "What do you mean?"

She said nothing, but looked at him pointedly, waiting for his response, willing him to be the one who spoke first.

"I don't know what you're talking about." But his voice sounded a little too defensive to be convincing.

"I heard you talking to Mr. Reeve, Will. I know what you did."

He glanced out of the room as if concerned that someone might overhear them. Then he stepped back into the room, quietly pulling the door closed behind him.

"Why are you treating Manny like this?" Hope demanded. "Why are you treating me like this— now, of all the times? What are you hiding?"

Will looked defiant. "I'm hiding nothing, Manny's possessed—he's mad, and he stole things from your guardian. By all accounts he's meddled in things he should've left well alone. If it leads him to trouble it's no more than he deserves." Will walked slowly across the room toward her, his voice agitated but deliberate.

"But I don't have a letter, Hope. Neither does Mr. Reeve. You've made a mistake." He looked round again, as if he wasn't confident they were alone. "And anyway I wasn't with Mr. Reeve this evening. He can tell you the same."

Will was very close to her now, whispering so that even if anyone else had been listening they wouldn't be able to hear what he said. "You don't know what you're meddling with. Stay away from us. Listen, I care about Manny, even if you don't think I do."

Will strode from the room. Hope heard the front door shut, and she sat down, staring at the darkened window in disbelief at the clumsiness of her confrontation.

Later that night, she lay awake in bed wondering what was to be done. She felt completely alone. Will was clearly taking the view that Manny deserved no forgiveness for his recent actions. And Will apparently would not be dissuaded on her account, either. Mr. Reeve was now against her, and her father was unable to help. She wondered briefly if she might confide in the housekeeper. But what use would that be?

She thought of Sister Aitkin and felt a pang of frustration. The Mormons had been so supportive and friendly, yet they were accused of deception and generally disliked by everyone Hope had come into contact with in the village. How could she go back to the Mormons? Yet she had felt such peace in their company and could not accept that they were as evil as people wanted to portray. In fact, it was those around her who had proven unreliable.

She reflected on her father's urging that she must trust her spirit. As she concentrated on this idea and what it meant for her, she grew increasingly convinced that she must act without delay and find Sister Aitkin.

The farmhouse was silent as Hope stepped down from the last stair and passed through the hallway toward the front door. The light had gone out in her guardian's bedroom, and she took it to mean that the housekeeper had now decided to sleep as well. Hope pulled open the door and shivered as cold air sucked through the gap. Her boots scraped against the step, a suddenly loud noise in the otherwise silent night. Holding her breath so she could listen more intently, she waited until she was sure the housekeeper had not been disturbed. The idea of venturing to Northwood in the dead of night was frightening, but something inside Hope drove her to keep going. No one in Ormley need know that she'd gone. She'd be back before dawn.

A barn owl swooped over the farm, something small gripped in its talons. Hope closed the door. Her arms stiffened, and a pain knotted at the base of her stomach. What if she couldn't wake Sister Aitkin? There was no one else to confide in. Hope wrapped the woolen shawl over her head and mouth. Her breath warmed the cloth as it leaked through, lingering around her head, drifting and dissolving into the darkness. She crept away.

Stars speckled the dome of the night sky. A cold wind swept across the bridle path and the shawl slapped at her face. She walked carefully, slowly, picking her way past the shadowy ruts, the stones and the potholes.

Then she stopped. Was there someone behind her? She listened, trying to work out what the noise had been, and then hurried on. Her imagination was scaring her. But her steps faltered as she strained to hear over the sound of her boots and the swish of her dress. She turned once more, clutching the edges of her shawl, peering into the darkness. An awful thought took hold of her. If she was attacked, no one could help. She mustn't think like that. Manny needed her help—he was in danger.

She bowed her head as she passed the taverns on Main Street. A drunken man stumbled out of one, falling toward her. Laughing, reeking of ale, he grabbed her arm, his unshaven, leering, stinking face pressed close to her. She pulled back and his grip tightened. Anger surged through her and she slapped him hard, twice. He cried out in surprise, his hands slipping as he recoiled, and she was able to pull loose. Although the anger had come in spite of her fear, she started to shake, and then she ran.

At the corner of West Road, a group of men watched her. She hurried past them and soon arrived at Sister Aitkin's house. She knocked loudly. Shivering and refusing to give in to the fear that made her want to look back at the men, Hope stood waiting, rubbing her arms.

After what seemed an age, the door opened, spilling light onto the street. It was Elder Armitage. Hope's smile faded. She resisted the immediate desire to barrack him, and instead concentrated on her need to help Manny. "Excuse me. I need to speak to Sister Aitkin. Please, I need to speak with her now."

The American blinked, scratching his head. He looked as if he'd been awakened, though he was still dressed in a suit. His shirt collar stuck out, his sleeves undone. He seemed to gather himself, peering out onto the street and then back at Hope. "Do you not know what time it is? It's past midnight!"

"Please, I need to speak to her."

Elder Armitage placed his hands on either side of the doorframe and then leaned forward, checking up and down the street again. Some men in the street jeered, and the missionary seemed to grasp the danger Hope had faced to come here. He ushered her in with a look of concern, and then said respectfully, "Give me a minute—you can sleep in the front room."

But Hope shook her head. "No. No, you don't understand. I don't want to stay—I can't. I must speak with Sister Aitkin. Please, would you just be kind enough to show me to her room?"

Elder Armitage looked doubtful but then acquiesced. "Wait here, I'll fetch you a candle."

Eleven

A Meeting of Minds

Although it wasn't long since the sounds of scuffling had died away, Manny knew the diversion had been a success, and for the first time since waking he felt relief. The struggle put up by the mysterious John had clearly taken the constables by surprise and required their complete attention. They'd been so occupied with arresting him that they had not even looked inside the hut. So far so good. Obviously they hadn't seen Manny when he opened the door. But they surely would have linked him with the hut now that John had taken the money. What had possessed him to do that?

On the other hand, it was possible John could be accused of having stolen it from him. In any case, if the police came back at all it would be likely not to be for a while. Manny thought it reasonable to suppose there were only the two officers on duty. The demands of their work required them to cover a large swath of the county, and it now played to his advantage. He was sure to have some time.

He crawled out from under the bed and brushed the dust from his hands. John had taken the money. He would be considered a vagrant and a thief, just as he, Manny, was considered a disturber of the peace and a thief. The police would now view them both as criminals, at least until he could retrieve the letter.

For a moment, he stood barefoot in the silence of the hut, having had no time even to put on his boots. He glanced around at the tiny room. It was just as well the constables hadn't entered; there would have been no means of escape. But this meeting with John had been for a reason. There were questions that needed answers, and there were answers that raised more questions. Manny began to search the hut, thinking about what was now required of him.

The simple fact was that John needed his help. And yet there was far more. Manny's compelling desire of yesterday—to leave the village—was now replaced with a new and exhilarating possibility. His father could actually be innocent. At first Manny could think only of the urgency of retrieving the letter, of proving the claim. His heart raced, and thoughts swirled in his mind. His father not guilty, Reeve guilty in his place?

After a few moments of elation at his father's possible innocence, Manny realized he must be cautious. There was no proof; he had only the word of a stranger who claimed to be Hope's long-lost father. But what reason did Manny have to doubt the claim? Had Edward Reeve truly been the one responsible for his own wife's death and Hope's mother's as well? Could this explain why they had never been permitted to speak of the past? Manny had never truly liked the mill owner, but was the man actually guilty of hiding so much? Why had no one discovered it before? Had Mr. Alderman known all of this, or only a part of it?

Manny was supposed to be searching for the letter. But even a cursory glance at the interior of this small shepherd's hut showed it was not here. He would need to return to the tarn. His mind kept coming back to the idea that his father could be innocent. The thought strengthened Manny. Yet without proof, he was further away than ever from gaining freedom from the pursuit of the law.

There was another thing. Manny knew Hope would want to know of her father's return, would want to see him, to discover his identity. But in the circumstances a safe reunion was out of the question. Nevertheless, Manny knew he must try to reunite her with her real father, let the consequence come.

Partly because it was so much to take in, and partly because the news was so sensational, Manny kept going over the memory of the encounter with John, of the sudden arrest. Doubt began to creep in again. Was it possible the man had lied to him? No. Manny rejected the idea quickly. What reason did he have to doubt he was telling the truth? He wondered again if it could be true that Reeve was responsible for his own wife's death.

As had been the case by the tarn the day before, it was difficult for Manny to think clearly, or to make much sense of what was happening. It was simply too much to take in.

Besides, he still needed the letter. Where was it? Mr. Alderman must have known something of all of this, but Manny was sure he couldn't have known the whole truth. Come to think of it, Manny argued to himself, how could John make such an accusation? And why had he taken so long to return? Never mind—the letter was all that mattered now. Manny must trust that reuniting Hope with her real father would help to vindicate them all. He must find the letter, and he must act swiftly as he'd been told to do. They must prove the truth of this claim to parentage, and they must prove that the money Manny had taken was rightfully his own.

He gathered some dirt, threw it over the fire, and then stopped. If the police did come back, they must not suspect that anyone else had been here. He suddenly felt very young and inexperienced. Pulling the sackcloth more tightly around his shoulders, he crept to the open door. He peeked out and stared at the place where the arrest had occurred, hearing again in his head the struggle. Now it almost seemed like a dream.

Manny tried hard to concentrate. Perhaps the letter had been dropped by the tarn. In any case he must get away from the hut before it was too late. He must not allow John's sacrifice to be in vain.

But he was famished, having not eaten since he'd left home. The bag he found tucked behind the chair held roasted chicken, a pile of crackers, and a metal cup. He ripped at the meat and shoved it into his mouth. Then he realized the food was a gift, so he must be respectful. He chewed more slowly, and then picked up the crackers, holding them almost reverently.

The surprise of the meeting and the shock of the news at the parting had shaken Manny, and I knew he longed to feel close to me. This was the opportunity I had been waiting for—the opportunity to reach him, to bring to his mind some memories that would prompt him about what was to be done. I knew the man's name troubled him. It was a name he felt oddly familiar with, and yet . . .

Nagged by curiosity, Manny sat hunched in the doorway, trying to remember. He knew that in order to understand why Hope's father's name troubled him, he first had to return in his mind to a place where he was small and scared and all alone.

I felt a surge of joy in the certain knowledge that he was prepared to try.

Swallowing the food in a determined gulp, Manny closed his eyes to draw the memories back.

I called his name, trying to extend my love, to give him encouragement.

I could see what he could see—he was a small boy again, standing by himself on the cobbles of The Fold, just beyond the doorstep in front of our house. He was trying not to cry, a graze on his hand, his trousers dusty and torn, blood dribbling over his knee. The door opens and I am there with him. I crouch down and reach out to pull him in, hold him tight to my chest.

Manny felt the wind leaking through the hut doorway, snapped open his eyes, and stared at the embers of the fire. The vision had come to him with power, the reality and peace of it leaving him in awe. It was as though he had been transported back in time to the very place he could see in his mind.

He pulled the sack away from his shoulders and bundled it up, then got to his knees, turning his head to the fire and drawing in the smell of the smoke. In his mind there was the heat of the bath, the stab of hot water as it touched the graze, steam rising into the kitchen.

I wipe his face. His mam, silent yet kindly, watches us from the corner of the room. The table is set for tea, and we are about to have our weekly family treat. The air is filled with the smell of baking bread and sausages and eggs, and mushrooms frying. We all love this tradition; it's been a weekly feast for as long as we can remember. But tonight it's different. It's Manny's birthday, so there's also a cake. Will waits, sitting, swinging his feet, smiling at me.

Manny winced at the thoughts, then rose and stumbled across the hut to the bed. He threw himself against it and held his hands tight, his fingers squeezed together, bone jamming on bone, knuckles pushed tight against his head. He buried his face in the blanket, praying, his knees turning cold on the hut floor.

And then he was back in his memory, in his bedroom, lying with me and Will and his mam. There's a candle, burning on the window ledge, like an all-seeing eye but we're all there safe, together.

"I reckon Ephraim's a great name, lad." I lean in, tuck him into bed, then look at Will and Lucy and we smile. "But I reckon Manny'll be easier for all of us to shout when it's time for his tea. What do you reckon? Anyhow, happy birthday, lad."

Manny smiles at me. I ruffle his hair and then blow out the light.

Manny opened his eyes. The embers of the fire were fading. The wind picked up, pulled through the doorway, and ghosted into the room, unsettling the ashes around his feet.

I called his name and he looked round. From the look of surprise I knew he thought he had heard me.

In his mind Manny heard thumps, the sound of someone banging at the front door of the house on The Fold. He saw himself stumble from his bed, reaching for the unlit candle, and staggering from the bedroom.

He is standing at the top of the stairs, and there is a voice. "A fire, Lucy—there's a fire! They're all trapped."

Chairs scrape against the kitchen floor; one falls back, is left laid across the ground.

A cold burst of air, the front door wide open.

The sky is lit by the throb of fire.

Lucy runs, dragging Manny, dragging Will into the darkness toward the mill. Other people run— shouting, screaming.

People are dying. People are in there dying. I am terrified for them.

Flames explode through the mill windows, glass spraying over the weavers below. Villagers at the courtyard gates shield their faces from the heat. A group of men, their dust-smeared faces shadowy beneath sweat-sodden hair, rush from the river with overfilled buckets; the sound of tramping clogs is everywhere. And I sprint, away from my children and my beautiful Lucy, across the courtyard to the great burning doors of the mill.

Manny sat, propped against the doorway, breathing the smell of the hut and the smell of smoldering ash. In his mind, he could see smoke curling into the night sky, then drifting across the moorland behind the mill.

I'm gulping the air as I stagger away from the burning building, holding a woman in my arms. It's Ellen Reeve, but my son can't see her face, and then I'm collapsing onto my knees and laying the woman down. My head is swimming from heat and suffocating smoke. Men swarm around me. I'm pushing myself up, distraught. There is no one else who knows where the others are, still trapped inside. And then Mr. Edward Reeve is there, pacing back and forth at the courtyard gates like a wounded tiger, his hands clasped tight behind his back. He's looking around—his face is white like a ghost—and he sees the woman lying listless on the cobbled ground. There is nothing, no hope in his eyes as he stumbles across the courtyard to reach me.

I look up and speak. "She's . . ."

But Mr. Reeve is waving me back, screaming like a man possessed. "I know why this happened, Isaac!" His voice is hoarse, breaking. "And you will pay."

I begin to protest, but he is deaf to my words. He cannot see reason. There are others still trapped, but he will not come back. He's away from me and falling, curled on the ground and sobbing—a grown man, a broken man who is now in mourning. And he will not come back.

I'm squinting at the crowd half-lit by the flames. I'm searching for my family. I know what is coming, and know I will do nothing else. Stumbling, I run to meet them, then reach through the cast-iron railings to grasp my wife's hand one last time. "Lucy, please take the boys back. This is no place for them or you."

Her gaze is bewildered. "How did this . . ."

"They're inside." I'm scared, knowing again what is about to be done. "I didn't know she and John were still in there." Gazing at Lucy, I plead for support, for some last balm of understanding. All I can see is her panic. I want to convey what I know I must do, but I cannot bring myself to utter the words. "Someone has . . ." I want to tell her I think Edward Reeve is responsible for killing his wife.

Horror passes over Lucy's face as she sees what I am about to do. She is desperate now, like a person is when there is nothing more that can be done. But we have no other choice.

"No . . ." She mumbles the protest through tears cascading over her face. "You've already tried . . ." Then one last panicked attempt to prevent me doing what we know must be done. "It's Manny's birthday, Isaac . . . think of our children."

I'm touching her mouth and trying to fix her eyes in my mind, trying to hold fast to our last few seconds, wanting to reach her, holding her hand. I look down at Manny and Will, then back at the fire. It's roaring now, and only I know where John and his wife will be. Ellen is dead, and I cannot let them die as well. Then I am telling her to go home. "Lucy," I say, looking down at the boys, "teach them the truth. I'll come back. I promise I'll come back." But I don't want to let them see this end of mine—this is no vision I want them to see.

She is clinging to me. I'm stroking her face. "Lucy, please. I must go."

She chokes back tears. And then angrily she turns away.

Without looking back I'm running into the mill, disappearing into the flames.

Twelve

Finding Truth, Finding Lies

Hope looked away as Sister Aitkin got out of bed. Although Hope did not fully grasp all that she herself was now struggling with, she felt the overwhelming weight her circumstances had thrust upon her, and still jumpy from the journey, she felt ready to break. Tightening her grip on the candle, she hissed her first question—"Why didn't you tell me?"

"Tell you what?" Sister Aitkin's face was obscured by the uneven light cast by the candle. The tone of her voice revealed that she was unnerved by the intrusion. The room felt cold.

"Why people hide things." Hope choked on the words.

Sister Aitkin's face became clearer as Hope held up the light. The woman looked confused, and then she frowned, as if she thought the conversation had taken a turn to the ridiculous. She put her hand to her head and squinted toward Hope. "What time is it? How did you get in?"

"Your man. Mr. Armitage."

Sister Aitkin's face flushed. The implication had clearly found its mark. "He's not my . . . he's a lodger, just as you were." Her voice rose. "What's happened to you? Why are you speaking to me like this?"

"Why didn't you tell me?"

"Tell you what?"

"About polygamy."

Sister Aitkin looked stunned. She might have been trying to guess what could possibly have brought Hope here in this condition, but by the expression on her face she had not been expecting this particular question.

"You see," Hope said softly, "you've done it too."

Sister Aitkin had the grace to be silent. They stared at each other for a minute. When Sister Aitkin spoke next, she was calmer and more earnest. "Yes, you're right. But there is much of our faith that we have not had time to discuss. I cannot take away your fears. I can only tell you that I know God has blessed me with the chance to become a Latter-day Saint, and that I have found happiness. Think of your baptism, Hope. Remember how you felt in your heart. Remember, Jesus said, 'By their fruits ye shall know them.'"

"But what if it's all a trick, an illusion?" Hope was shaking so hard she had to sit down. In spite of the converging distress she wasn't really angry with Sister Aitkin. She now began to feel ashamed for being so rude as to storm in like this, demanding answers in such an aggressive way. She slumped on the bed, all of the tension she had been carrying since the baptism suddenly threatening to burst out of her in a flood of tears.

Sister Aitkin reached out and held Hope's hand. The contact was reassuring. Hope's hostility had only come of desperation. She felt a little better.

"There's a scripture," Sister Aitkin said gently, "that contains within it a message that has helped me many times, especially when I've wondered about the truth of the things I committed myself to. I took these words to heart; they're written in my soul. Let me share them with you now." She was silent for a moment, then read, "'O then, is not this real? I say unto you, yea; because it is light; and whatsoever is light, is good.'"

She opened her eyes and paused again, as if she wanted Hope to register the significance of the words. "You cannot always be sure of knowing why and how. There are men and philosophies that will always oppose us. But you can let the light that comes of faith shine inside of you."

Sister Aitkin picked up an open book that had lain unnoticed next to Hope on the dresser. "Now read this." Sister Aitkin offered the book to her as if it were a peace offering and smiled encouragingly for her to take it.

Although she hadn't seen the cover, Hope knew this was a copy of the Book of Mormon. She looked at the words Sister Aitkin had pointed to, took the book in her trembling hands, and read softly, "'Now we will compare the word unto a seed. Now if ye give place, that a seed may be planted in your heart, behold, if it be a true seed, or a good seed, if ye do not cast it out by your unbelief, that ye will resist the spirit of the Lord, behold, it will begin to swell within your breasts; and when ye feel these swelling motions, ye will begin to say within yourselves, It must needs be that this is a good seed, or that the word is good, for it beginneth to enlarge my soul; yea, it beginneth to enlighten my understanding, yea, and it beginneth to be delicious to me.'"

Hope understood. These scriptures gave her a way to keep trying. They gave her consolation, and she began to feel a greater sense of peace, more so than she had done even at her baptism. She knew her mind had been enlightened, and she knew these feelings could help her in the future. It was as though a light had come on inside her, and intense relief came suddenly. "I want to believe," she said. "But my guardian is close to death and delirious. Manny is gone. And Will and Mr. Reeve . . ."

"I'm so sorry," Sister Aitkin said simply.

"I think my father was trying to tell me something this evening," Hope explained. "But he has a fever and cannot converse properly."

"I can't give you all the answers you want," Sister Aitkin said. "I don't have them all. But I do know God hears my prayers. I can only tell you to trust your spirit. You mustn't be afraid."

Hope looked down thoughtfully. "That's what my father said. 'Trust your spirit.' And I am trying to, I really am. But what am I to do about Will? He's hiding a letter from me and pretending he hasn't got it. I know Manny is falsely accused."

"What do you mean?"

"There's a letter—from Father, I think. I overheard Will talking to Mr. Reeve about it earlier. They said it was for me. But they don't want me to see it."

Sister Aitkin nodded and then took a deep breath as if she was about to say something significant. She took Hope's hand. "Come and speak with Elder Armitage. There's news he needs to tell you."

When they walked into the sitting room, Elder Armitage turned to face Hope. He wore such a look of compassion that she wondered how she could have doubted his sincerity.

"I was standing at the side of the docks," he began, "watching the shipping, contemplating the great work that had commenced here in England, when a man approached me. He seemed uncertain about speaking with me at first, as if he wasn't sure about asking my name. I could see he was a sailor. After a time he enquired about my faith, and I informed him that I was a Latter-day Saint. He seemed greatly encouraged by this and asked me if I could try to find a certain George Alderman. I asked him what it was about, but he swore me to secrecy. He instructed me where to go, saying that Mr. Alderman had been friendly to the Mormons once. And then he asked if I could deliver a gift.

"He specifically asked me to find out about you, Miss Alderman, though he asked me to keep the knowledge of his presence a secret. As you are now aware I did all of these things, but upon leaving Ormley, I felt compelled to speak with your friend, young Manny Shaw."

Hope tried to stay calm, but her mind was in a flurry. She thought of the inscription at the front of the Bible—*A gift for a gift*—and what possible reason a man, a stranger from the seas, could have for getting in touch with her like this. Then with a thrill of excitement, she wondered if the man Elder Armitage had met might be her father. The thought was almost too exciting to take in.

"He claimed to have lived in England around the time Queen Victoria ascended to the throne—1837," Elder Armitage went on. "He believed the village unsafe for him to come back to."

"Why? Who would object to his return?" But Hope knew the answer before she had even finished the question. "What could Mr. Reeve have against me knowing my real father?"

Elder Armitage looked at Sister Aitkin. "In view of the circumstances, Miss Alderman, I think we should inform the police. To withhold such knowledge from them would be a mistake, a misdeed."

Hope shook her head. "I have no evidence. Will is refusing to admit to it. You only have my word. I need to go back to Ormley. I need to think about what to do."

"Why don't you stay here for the night?" Sister Aitkin offered. She said it pleasantly, but there was firmness in her voice. "It cannot be safe for you to be out at this time."

"I can't." Hope didn't want to admit that the true reason for this sudden leaving was an impetuous desire to retrieve the lost letter from Mr. Reeve's home. "It's not safe for me to stay here any longer than I must." She stood up and made for the door. "I need to go home."

Sister Aitkin looked unsure. "Wait a while—take some sleep and leave at daybreak."

"No, I can't. Really, I understand that you fear for my safety, but I cannot risk being discovered to have been away . . ." Hope's voice trailed off.

Sister Aitkin was unconvinced. "Elder Armitage, what have you to say on the matter?"

The American had been watching Hope all the while, his eyes narrowed shrewdly as if he was working out what she really meant to do. "Well, one thing is certain, the poor girl will not be safe, either if she stays or if she should go. Therefore, I propose to escort her back to the village under cover of night."

Sister Aitkin looked shocked. "But, sir, you are expected in Liverpool, and early. You must get some sleep as well."

"Dear lady, we cannot stand by and leave Miss Alderman in such dire circumstances. I shall survive without one night of sleep. How do you think I managed to cross the Atlantic?" Hope was sure she detected a note of jest in his voice.

Sister Aitkin looked as if she might still protest, then nodded and followed Hope out into the hallway. "All the same I'd feel a great deal happier if you stayed. It'll not be good for you to be out at this time."

"I know. Thank you. And thank you for helping me. I'm sorry I was so rude to you."

For a reply Sister Aitkin reached out, took Hope in her arms again, and hugged her tight. "If you need to come back, do so without hesitation."

Hope thanked her, then stepped out into the night and covered her hair with her shawl. She and the missionary hurried away.

———⊶⊷———

Hope shifted her weight, her skin clammy beneath damp clothes. She was grateful Elder Armitage had not insisted on staying with her longer, that he'd had to return to Liverpool. With surprise she realized it was now Wednesday, the twenty-first day of the month, already two days since her baptism. Her eyes stung from lack of sleep, and her muscles ached. She wondered if she had the nerve to do what she planned.

Mr. Reeve's manor was wreathed in early morning mist, the grounds enclosed by a high red-brick wall. A simple wooden gate barred her way into the garden. But it was early. She could creep into the grounds, hide in the shrubbery, and watch for her chance to break in. She felt a little guilty knowing she had been less than honest with Sister Aitkin about her intentions. She wondered at the task she had set herself—how she would even begin to locate the letter.

The gate swung open silently and easily. In front of the low-set mullioned windows of Mr. Reeve's house was a perfectly cut, perfectly square privet hedge. Hope looked around at the rest of the garden. Although she had grown up in the village she had never been inside the grounds of this house, and the strangeness of her reason for being here now—as a prospective housebreaker—made her feel oddly separated from her surroundings. It seemed as though she had stepped into another world, as if Ormley itself no longer existed. She could hear nothing but the song of a single lark. The grass was well kept and heavy with dew. Obviously Mr. Reeve liked to keep a meticulous lawn. Shrubs grew up by the walls, and there were no flowers anywhere except in the center of the lawn where a single red rose bush had been planted. Around the base of the flower lay many faded petals.

Hope hid behind the rhododendrons. A spider's web caught against the side of her face, and she slipped as she tried to wipe it away. Looking down, she saw mud staining the hem of her dress. Mud was caked around the soles of her boots as well, and she began wiping off as much of it as she could. If she was to get into the house, there must be no evidence to give her away. She rubbed her arms and then breathed on her hands, trying to control her anxiety. Where was Manny, and what was he doing? What else could Hope do now, apart from wait for her chance?

Something flapped behind her, and she spun around in alarm to see what had made the noise. But it was just a sparrow. Still, Hope was trembling. She must act—time was running out. People would soon notice she was missing. She wiped the last of the mud from her boots and hurried across the garden, onto a gravel path and over the box hedge. Peering in through one of the windows, she made out a bookcase and decided this room was the library. At the sound of the front door opening, she ducked instinctively. There was only one option if she was to hide: the privet hedge. It was low, but by lying very flat and very still on the ground, she could just about be sure to be hidden. She heard footsteps coming down the stairs from the house, then fading as the person walked away over the gravel.

Hope waited, wondering how long it would be until it was safe to move. Then she heard the person return and stride back up the steps. The door closed but there was no sound of a lock being turned. Hope waited just a moment longer, crept out from her hiding place, and followed.

Mr. Reeve's entrance hall was cold, airy, and dimly lit. Hope suspected it had once been alive with voices. Light would have flowed in abundance, and the house would have been always warm. But after his wife's death, Mr. Reeve was said to have sent almost all of his servants away. Only a few remained, and they rarely mixed with anyone from the village.

The hallway floor was stone, and on the far side was a polished mahogany staircase. Hope heard the agitated shouts of women, and then the clatter of pans. Guessing Mr. Reeve's breakfast was being prepared, Hope held her breath and listened for the sound of anyone approaching, but doors slammed and the voices and clattering died away. In a corner of the entrance hall, a grandfather clock ticked offbeat with her heart. A large oil painting of a ship in a storm hung on the wall opposite her. Upstairs, a door clicked shut. She looked around quickly for a place to hide. With the entrance hall so bare, the only real possibility lay through an open door on her left. Through the gap of the open door, she could see a well-kept room and hear a fire spitting and crackling in the grate. Stepping closer, she recognized the bookcase she'd seen from outside. The library.

Hope looked in carefully and found that no one was there. The smell of the fire suggested it had only just been lit. Perhaps Mr. Reeve was planning to breakfast in here. She wondered about the wisdom of investigating the room but then hurried inside.

In shadow, in the corner of the room, were two large marble statues—one a soldier playing a fife, and the other an army officer, standing as if posing for a portrait. They would be large enough to hide behind if she was disturbed. Holding her skirt to stop it from catching on anything, Hope tiptoed quickly through the room, looking for any sign of papers or letters. She must be quiet and she must be patient, but she must not delay.

Thirteen

Getting Near the Truth

Edward Reeve always sought attention. A keen socialite, he was gregarious, quick to invite others into his house. He was a center around which others revolved, a magnet, popular to a fault—talking often of his interests in the local economy, speaking earnestly with his workers, eager to understand their situation.

He was a good man. He wouldn't admit to it, but I knew he enjoyed the high esteem in which he was held. He cultivated it, and he confided in me more than once that he knew that should he lose the faith of his workforce, his days in manufacturing would be numbered. He was a philanthropist, a popular employer. It was no wonder people closed ranks around him after I died. His style of employment had always been a startling contrast to the grim tales coming out of some of the larger cities and towns. It was little wonder that people had moved to our village in order to gain work. Reeve paid well, treated well, and was known near and far as a kind and good-natured gentleman.

Of course it was little wonder that the villagers never pursued nor sought an inquiry into the true circumstances surrounding the fire. They simply had sympathy for Mr. Reeve's tragic loss and acknowledged it with a dutiful silence. There was enough information to claim that I was a troublemaker. But they had not known that he had always possessed a serious flaw. He was addicted to gambling.

I learned of this vice shortly after his return from London, soon after my attempt to help him read the Book of Mormon, and when his sudden loss of light was most pronounced. "I am ruined," was all he would say. He had cursed it under his breath, unaware I was hearing his lament. He'd been in a curt mood for a couple of days when I ventured to ask him what the matter was. He promptly retorted by threatening me with the loss of my job if I didn't give up my interest in the Mormons. But he hadn't been serious. He apologized and asked if he might confide in me. In me? Imagine it. He said he liked Lucy and me too well to destroy our living. And then he proceeded to say that on account of the fact that we'd been such loyal friends he felt he might trust me with some private affair. I was flattered by this confidence, and a few days after ventured to ask him if he would become a godfather to my children. I had never been sure of the doctrine of child baptism, but supposed that to have a link with Edward might serve my children well. At first he'd seemed immensely pleased at the idea. Perhaps it was one reason he took a continuing interest in the family after my death. Certainly everyone knew of his fondness for Will and Manny, and I suppose continuing to be charitable enabled him to prove his respectability in the eyes of the law. His regular visits after my death were accompanied by small donations of credit and food. However, the christenings never transpired.

But to return to the confidence he wished to share with me. In short it was this: Reeve and his wife Ellen were facing great financial hardship, brought on by his inability to stop playing cards. Initially, he apologized for his bad treatment of me and assured me that I would always have work, but then he acknowledged that his trips to London had not only been on business but to play for higher and higher stakes. He was at a complete loss about what to do.

The sun was rising over the moorland, casting a faint blood-red light into the cloud. Above the moors, a kestrel hovered as if held by an invisible thread. Manny knelt, watching it, willing it loose. After leaving the shepherd hut, he'd made his way straight back to the tarn, where he'd slept only a little waiting for dawn. The memories of the night were still with him, and he felt certain his father's death had been abused by Reeve. In Manny's mind he heard men shout, saw flames bursting through the mill roof. Weavers gathering by the water wheel, gesturing, waving as if to urge someone to jump. Two bodies falling from high up, out from the side of the mill, and then disappearing into the river. Men crowding the riverbank, pulling a body out from the water. Distant shouts cascading over the courtyard, running men yelling the words "It's Isaac. Isaac Shaw's dead."

Manny looked into the tarn. Accepting the vision of his father's death was somehow healing. He felt that his mind was clear, his heart open and teachable. He hungered for truth.

Let go of your hurt.

The words came to him just as they had outside the mill. But this time he understood the invitation more quickly and let it gain strength in his heart. He thought he heard a sound behind him and spun round to see who was there.

By the look of surprise on Manny's face, I knew he could see me. I smiled at him and pointed toward the water, hoping he might understand my message. I sought his help in providing me with vicarious baptism, yet I also wanted to impress upon him the rightness of his desire to be a better man. All the time I had been there with him, Manny had barely moved. Then his lips mouthed, "Dad?"

I saw the hope growing in his eyes, renewed energy and strength to be true and decent and honorable flowing back into his heart. I wasn't able to speak to him yet, only to begin to prepare his mind for the purpose for which I had originally called him those few days before. I looked into his innocent, childlike eyes and wished I could hold him tight again. But instead, I allowed myself to retreat from his view and called to him by the Spirit once more: "Do not hate Edward. Only do what is right."

It is strange to say that in spite of the wrong he had done to my family, I myself bore no ill will to my former employer. I pitied him and knew that Manny must also; indeed, he must come to have compassion both for himself and for Reeve, if he was to make himself right to enjoy communion with his Father in heaven.

Manny looked down, overwhelmed by the vision he'd had, and then allowed himself to bask in the relief it brought. In the rushing surge of hope and peace and strength, he marveled at what he had seen. He wondered at the way his promptings had led to a vision of his father, rejoiced at the path he had taken, and was humbled by the greater insight it had given him. How had he become so fortunate?

Suddenly he knew he must return quickly to the village. All he'd wanted was the freedom to leave the mill behind, to run away with Hope and to live life as he chose—a life of freedom. He'd wanted to be a good man, to prove he lived with integrity and respectability. Perhaps it had been foolish to dream of standing on the deck of a tall ship and sailing out of Liverpool, and to be wedded to Hope in this way. But since he suspected Reeve of deceit, and knowing as he did the craving Hope felt to know the identity of her father and mother, and that more than anything she would long to speak with John, there was no way Manny could turn away from what must be done. And here in the wilderness of the moorland, he finally came to see that his father was with him, had always been with him, and had helped him in his quest for truth.

This simple fact alone gave Manny far greater confidence than he had ever known, and he felt to bless the circumstances that had brought him here. A comforting thought occurred to him. He had imagined that giving up his freedom by turning himself into the police would mean the loss of happiness, but instead of grief he felt only exhilaration and peace.

He thought how odd it was that at this moment of willingly submitting to whatever might come from this choice, he felt freer. He had always imagined that the decision to stop fighting, to face his fate and allow it to take him wherever it chose, would have been a weight—not this deep sense of power.

Nevertheless, he still needed to make certain the letter was gone. There was a limit to the number of places it might be. Maybe he'd dropped it somewhere near Mr. Alderman's farmhouse. But Manny had held both the envelope and the money here at the tarn.

He mused on the consequences of losing something as small and seemingly insignificant as a letter, and he acknowledged wryly the value of a few written words. What if the police had it? Why hadn't he thought of that before? The police might even think Hope's father had robbed him.

Or perhaps Will had it. Because Manny knew that Mr. Alderman had not wished the letter read by anyone before Obadiah Thomas, this possibility troubled him greatly. But he reasoned that his brother couldn't read and that, even if he did have the letter, it was unlikely he'd let anyone else know.

What if it was in the tarn, buried with the vase? If it was, it was sure to be ruined. But damaged evidence was better than none at all. And it was worth trying. Manny took off his coat. There was one more thing he must do.

He knelt down and then, a little hesitantly, closed his eyes. "I thank thee for sending me Dad. I know I've not always been as good as you might want me to be. I'm sorry. Please help me now. I know I'll need strength."

Manny waited for a few moments, his head still bowed, trying to hold onto the feeling of concentration and sincerity. He recalled his baptism and remembered Hope, her hair and clothes still wet from the river, her face radiant, people clapping, moving away, and then his attempt to propose.

For the first time since the baptism, he thought of the counsel Elder Armitage had been so eager to share. "I want to teach you a doctrine," the missionary had said, opening his Bible, "that I hope will guide you if you are ever in doubt about the worth of what you have done here today. In the twentieth chapter of the book of John, the Lord blessed the disciples, almost immediately following his resurrection. The words he spoke are recorded here: 'Receive ye the Holy Ghost.'" Elder Armitage had smiled encouragingly as he asked, "What were the disciples doing before the Lord said those words?"

Manny hadn't known.

"Then I'll tell you. They were hiding. Now, let's go forward in time, about six weeks, say, to the second chapter of Acts. 'And there appeared unto them cloven tongues like as of fire . . . And they were all filled with the Holy Ghost, and began to speak with other tongues, as the Spirit gave them utterance . . . Now when this was noised abroad, the multitude came together, and were confounded, because that every man heard them speak in his own language.'" Elder Armitage had snapped shut the Bible. "When you give yourself to the Lord without qualification, when you serve him with faith, with the courage to act no matter the consequence, you receive the influence and power of Holy Ghost. And miracles happen! Peter was imprisoned, but the Lord released him. Stephen was killed, but in death he saw God. John was exiled, but in captivity he received the word of God. To the man who acts with faith, the Holy Ghost will surely come!"

———

Manny stared at his reflection in the surface of the water. He must make sure the letter was not in the tarn. His shirt and trousers were piled neatly by his feet. In his heart, he knew what this act of searching represented. Through his vision he knew it was no coincidence that so much had taken place by the tarn. He looked out over the wild, open moorland.

He would begin again, with renewed determination, and he would find Hope. Here, this morning, he would begin to do whatever it took to show her that he loved her. No matter what happened. No matter what people would think. He would stop running away, and Hope would know he loved her.

Manny took a deep breath and dived into the tarn. The water was so cold it felt was as though he was swimming in ice, so cold that at first he thought he would not bear it. Then he writhed, pulling and willing himself down and reached out, sweeping his hands through the darkness, searching the stones and the silt until his lungs burned for air.

He burst out of the water, clenching his teeth to stop them from chattering. Perhaps the vase had sunk somewhere nearer to the center. He waded deeper, his body already beginning to numb. He kept wading until the water was over his shoulders. He was past shivering now and his toes stubbed against something smooth and solid. He turned, peering down through the water, feeling around with his toe. He'd found it. He dived again. Seizing the vase with both hands, he tugged it loose and checked inside. It was empty. The icy cold of the water made his fingers stiff and clumsy. He dropped the vase back onto the tarn's bed, and willing himself on for just a little longer, he kept turning over stones and searching the silt. Eventually, when his lungs and body could bear it no longer, and thoroughly satisfied the letter was not there, he pushed up to the surface.

Finally he understood. It mattered not if the letter was gone; in Manny's heart he knew he could take its message. He could return to Hope and tell her himself, and he could testify as to John's innocence with regard to the money. Manny knew it would lead to his own arrest. But there would be no cause for them both to be jailed.

It felt right, and it was right. He loved Hope. For the first time since his baptism, he had begun to understand his commitment to follow Jesus, and this understanding encouraged him.

He was ready to go to Northwood.

———∞∞∞———

Manny banged on Sister Aitkin's door and stood back to wait. If there was no one here, he must quickly find another way to locate Obadiah Thomas's office and return to Ormley. Surely Hope had gone there if she was no longer here. Perhaps she was already confused by the delay in his return and had gone back to the village. He imagined she would have been persuaded against him. That being the case, he must bear his witness and trust in the Lord. Manny must be strong for her, even if she no longer believed him to be innocent. He tried to imagine how she would have reacted to the news of Mr. Alderman's accident, to the news of Manny's running away, and wondered how best to give her the news of her father, John.

The sunlight on the front window dulled. Several sheets of newspaper were scattered across the cobbles, and a breeze lifted and carried them away down the street.

Hearing laughter behind him, Manny turned and saw a group of children running and playing. They skipped past him and waved and smiled. He smiled back and then banged on Sister Aitkin's door again. His knuckles stung and he rubbed the back of his hand. They'd taken him in before—surely they would again. He peered through the window. This was the right house, he was sure of it. He knocked again, harder. The door opened a little and Sister Aitkin's face appeared in the gap.

"I've come back for Hope," he said.

"Manny? Manny Shaw? Where have you been?"

"Please, where is Hope?"

Sister Aitkin looked troubled and then, looking past Manny as if she expected someone to be listening, whispered, "Come in."

"What is it?"

"Come in," Sister Aitkin repeated. She opened the door and gestured for Manny to enter.

"Where's Elder Armitage?"

"He's away to Liverpool." She ushered Manny into the hallway and closed the door. "He had to leave this morning. Follow me—I need to tell you what happened." She walked silently toward the parlor, and he had no option but to follow.

When he had taken a seat, Sister Aitkin came straight to the point. "Hope came to see me last night."

"What? Why? What did she say? Is she safe?"

"She said your brother was hiding a letter."

Manny's heart sank.

"But Hope believes he's falsely accused you. She was concerned for your safety."

This at least offered some comfort. Hope was not against Manny then. "Has— has she seen the letter?" he asked.

"No."

"Then where is it?"

"She said Mr. Reeve had it." Sister Aitkin looked flustered by Manny's question, as if she felt guilty about something. "I think she's so set on finding out her parents' identity that she might try to break into Mr. Reeve's house to find the letter. I tried to make her stay here, but . . ."

Manny remembered John's warning that Mr. Reeve would destroy any proof of his return. "I came to tell Hope I've found her real father. That he's been arrested. The letter was evidence that he's her father."

Looking distraught, Sister Aitkin related all that Elder Armitage had disclosed to Hope during the night. Then she said, "Manny, you have to do something. Go to the police."

"I can't—not yet. I need to tell Hope that her father is near."

"But Mr. Reeve and your brother are breaking the law."

"I know. But I can't prove that."

"But you can't just leave her to them. She went back, partly for your sake, not just for herself."

"I know. Sister Aitkin, there's someone else— someone Hope's guardian implored me to find."

"What do you mean?"

"Mr. Alderman and Hope's real father both gave me the name of a man who lives here in Northwood. Perhaps you've heard of him? His name is Obadiah Thomas. I think he can help us." Manny felt an inexplicable thrill of fear at the thought of going to someone who dealt in law. "He's a solicitor."

Sister Aitkin's face brightened. "Yes, I know. There's a little street called New Court—it's off

Main Street, about halfway down on the left. He has an office there, opposite the bookseller." Then she seemed concerned again. "But Manny, there's no evidence. You'll be—"

"Hope must be assisted," Manny said before the woman could finish. "I shall swear to what I've seen. Besides, I believe Reeve is guilty of some crime himself. It may be difficult to prove, but I cannot hide away when I might prove helpful. Anyway, Hope will need a defense if she has broken into Mr. Reeve's house. We can challenge him if we vouch for her reasons." Manny stood and made for the door, but then stopped with an idea that had just occurred to him. "Sister Aitkin?"

She looked up at him.

"Will you go to Obadiah Thomas for me? Will you tell him all that you have learned? Perhaps he can help us now."

She nodded.

$\mathcal{F}$ ourteen

Into the Fire

The fire in the library spat and crackled. Hope had been fortunate. Mr. Reeve had come back so quietly that she heard him only at the last second, but she had been close enough to the statues to hide. Now, from her hiding place, she could see him slumped in his chair, reading a letter. He looked tired. There was something else, an eerie strangeness about the room. It felt unlived in, and yet . . . Something in the contrast between Mr. Reeve's defeated repose and a freshly burning fire struck her forcefully, as if it held more meaning than she could quite understand. She watched as he stared at the letter in his hand and then sat back, lost in his thoughts, gazing out through the half-open window shutters.

A soft morning light streamed into the library, a brightness and strength quite at odds with the room, but Mr. Reeve seemed oblivious to it. After several long minutes, he thoughtfully tapped the arm of his chair, put the letter on the desk, and left the room, shutting the door quietly behind him.

Hope was caught in two minds. Should she take advantage of Reeve's absence, or should she wait to see if this was only a brief departure? How long must she wait before she could assume it safe to emerge? She waited. But the chimes of the clock for the three-quarter hour passed and he still did not return. Each passing minute seemed wasted, and the longer she hesitated, the more chance she had of being caught. The thought of discovering the message from her guardian almost drove her to distraction.

There was a letter just a few paces away. Surely it was the same one she sought—and yet this hesitation. Perhaps the reality of knowing a thing for sure, rather than only wishing one could find the answer, explained this delay. But suddenly she resolved her indecision. If she waited any longer she might lose her chance altogether. She squeezed past the statues, hurried across the room, and picked up the letter.

The writing was not her father's. Discouraged, she put the letter down. Then a phrase caught her attention. Curious to understand its meaning, she picked up the letter again, wondering who it was from. It was the end of what appeared to be a much longer letter. She looked for any other sheets but could find nothing, and what she had in her hands made little sense.

*Darling, I am thrilled to be able to tell you
this now. I know it is what you have always*

*craved and what you have always hoped
for. As we sailed from India, I thought we
might never know this joy.*

The name signed at the end looked like Ellen.

The library door opened behind Hope, and she
turned quickly. It was Mr. Reeve. She stepped
away from the table, still holding the letter.
Suddenly her impetuous attempt to find the other
letter seemed the most foolish thing she could ever
have thought to do. She was caught in the act of
housebreaking.

There would be shame on her father, sensation
in the village, the law to face, and Reeve still in
control of the facts she most needed. She began
to speak hastily. "I— you— I'm sorry . . . I don't
know what came over me. I shouldn't have come
here. I . . ."

But Mr. Reeve did not look shocked at her
presence, nor did he seem angry. Instead, he
glanced out into the hallway as if he would rather
his servants did not know of Hope's arrival. Then
he slowly closed the door.

She started forward but he raised his hand,
smiling gently, as if to calm her. He seemed amused
by her alarm.

"Don't be afraid," he said softly. "I'm not angry
with you. You belong here. I have been remiss in not
inviting you here before. Please, sit down. I assure
you I am not angry. You're frightened. I know you've
suffered a great deal. Please, let me help you."

Willing herself to act calm and trying to
take in this unexpected response, Hope placed

the letter back on the table. Mr. Reeve must know what she was seeking, and yet he seemed different, sincere, unconcerned by her presence. But something about the way he looked at her made her feel deeply uneasy. There was a kind of wide-eyed haste in his gaze that she had not seen before. He walked over to the desk and picked up the letter. Looking down at it, he seemed to be choosing his words carefully. "I am surprised by your behavior, but I'm not angry."

He turned and smiled at her. "You see, I saw you hiding across the lawn. I asked my butler to unlock the door. Much has happened in Ormley over the past few days. I fear there is change coming, and that there is little I can do to prevent it now. You are not the only one in need of comfort." He turned sadly and faced the window. "I can scarcely believe that I have never asked you here before."

"I'm sorry, sir," Hope said, praying she didn't sound as alarmed as she felt. "I don't know what came over me. I shouldn't have broken in. I shouldn't have pried. I thought . . . Forgive me." She made to leave.

Mr. Reeve raised his hand, dismissing her apology. He turned and approached slowly, then reached out and clamped hold of her arm. "You see, in so many ways we are alike. We are more connected by fate than you could possibly know. We both long to be enlightened, we have both been misjudged. And we are both alone. We are more connected than you know. And I suspect that, like me, you wish we were not as we have turned out."

If Hope had suspected he was beginning to lose his mind, she was now sure of it. His voice was all reason, calm and unflustered, and yet he was making very little sense. His determination not to admit to being surprised or outraged about her presence in his home left her baffled and unnerved. But it wouldn't do to run away from her purpose now, so she mustered her courage. "I heard you talking to Will yesterday evening."

Mr. Reeve looked at her shrewdly. "And so you came seeking the letter from your guardian. I knew you were listening. I've been expecting you to come. Wait here." He left the room.

Hope felt confused and then even more afraid. Mr. Reeve was far too welcoming, too calm. In all her life she had never known him to act this way toward her. Her face felt hot with anxiety. She must not show her fear.

She looked around the library and then walked over to the statue of the army officer. The face resembled Mr. Reeve's, though the eyes seemed younger. And somehow more content.

There was a polite cough behind her, and she turned quickly.

"Excuse me," said Mr. Reeve. He was the model of courtesy. He pointed at the statue of the man playing the fife. "He's remarkably like me, don't you think? And yet it is not me. He was my brother."

Hope wasn't sure what to say, but looking at the figures she could see the resemblance.

"You are the first visitor to have stepped into this room in over sixteen years." He held up a white satin gown. "Incidentally, I understand from

William that you might have been planning to marry. If so, I should be glad to give you this as a gift. Perhaps you might like to try it on? I've called one of my servants to help you."

Hope felt the blood rise in her cheeks. Mr. Reeve was being far too familiar. He was going insane. His friendliness was forced, unnatural.

"Thank you," she said, trying to sound gracious. "It is very good of you. But I should be grateful if you'd let me leave now. I think I should return to my guardian." She tried to hold herself erect and dignified, knowing she must look as dirty and bedraggled as she felt.

Reeve looked mildly offended, then amused again. "You don't trust me, do you?" He held up the letter. "But I thought you wanted to see this."

"I'd like to know what you have against me knowing about my real father," Hope retorted.

"You know I could have you arrested?" Mr. Reeve said. He spoke it softly, but there was a dangerous edge to his voice. "You understand that I am allowing you to remain here as my guest. I know you better than you suppose. Please do not reject my hospitality."

A maid emerged in the doorway. "You called for me, sir." She looked at Hope and then back at Mr. Reeve, evidently surprised to see her master with a young woman.

His calmness returned and he draped the dress over a chair. He turned to the maid and waved her away. "No. Not now. Leave us. I have everything in hand. I shall call you should Miss Alderman change her mind."

"Pardon me, sir," the maid said, a little flustered, "but the butler says there's a gentleman outside as is insisting on seeing you. He expressly asked about the whereabouts of a certain letter."

Mr. Reeve looked dismayed, suddenly out of control, and his face hardened. He looked as if he might do something dangerous. Hope looked at the maid and a sudden mad impulse seized her. It felt reckless but the words came out before she could stop them. "The letter belongs to me, miss. Mr. Reeve's lying to us all. He's been hiding it. And now he's holding me here against my will. Please, you must inform the constable."

Mr. Reeve stiffened, color rising in his face. He glanced back to where the maid stood waiting. "I'll see to the young woman. I think she's suffering delusions." He waited for the maid to leave and then took hold of Hope's arm and steered her out of the library. He leaned in closer. "I'd rather you didn't behave like this, Miss Alderman. I do know why it is you're looking for that letter. But you may find you'd have rather not known."

"That's for me to decide!" Hope shouted. The maid was walking away across the hall, looking back, obviously unnerved. "Please, don't leave," Hope called. The maid glanced back again and then hurried away.

Mr. Reeve leaned in close again. "I'm not afraid of your judgment, Miss Alderman. But I can't let you go about creating fear and pain for everybody else. Words can change a person's heart, you know."

The man's cryptic threats made no sense. "Just give me the letter," Hope shouted.

"Don't shout," Mr. Reeve said. "You'll disturb the servants."

"Let me go."

"They'll think you should be arrested," he replied, smiling in a maddeningly superior way.

She pulled away from him.

"You know, I'm glad you came here." He suddenly reached out and grabbed her arm again. "I'd been trying to decide what to do. Our time here is running out. I've tried to believe I could outlive the past, but I can't. Don't blame me when you know . . ." There was a faint trace of sweat on his brow. "I've made up my mind," he said. "I want you to come with me."

Hope squirmed, trying to loosen from his grasp, but he was too strong. She could smell his stale sweat. She began to panic. "Sister Aitkin and Elder Armitage know I'm here. They know why I'm here as well."

"Come now, don't be aggressive, Miss Alderman. And why would you listen to them? What do they know about grief? Besides, I can tell you the truth about Mormons. I can tell you who you are." He placed his hand on her mouth, and looked round as if to make sure they would not be overheard. "You remind me so much of your *aunt*. And you're beautiful, just as Ellen was. I would have been content to live in a pauper's house, if only she'd stayed with me."

Mr. Reeve pulled Hope upstairs, the old wood of the staircase creaking as they climbed. On the landing, they turned down a narrow carpeted passageway. He stopped outside a closed door, fished a key from his pocket, and turned the lock. "There are aspects of your past that you do not understand." He ushered her through the now-open door.

The room was small. To the right of Hope was a four-poster bed. From the smell of the room it was clear it had been left unchanged for many years. There were cobwebs and dust everywhere, and an overwhelming smell of mustiness. Opposite her, set in the window, were hundreds of pieces of red-and-green stained glass that outlined the image of an elegant woman, dressed in a white gown similar to the one Mr. Reeve had brought to the library for Hope to try on. But this woman also held an umbrella and wore a silk scarf draped around her shoulders.

"Now, let me explain to you," said Mr. Reeve, giving the window portrait barely a glance. "Let me tell you about the parasitic Shaw family." He pulled a framed picture from a drawer and held it up to the light. It was a portrait of Mr. Reeve and the woman in the stained-glass window, and there was another finely dressed man with an equally handsome woman.

Hope immediately saw the resemblance to herself. With a sudden awful sinking feeling that should have been joy in any other circumstance, she knew she was looking at her mother.

"You'll be glad to be free of the Shaws' influence. It was Isaac Shaw's fault that Ellen left me, just as it was Isaac Shaw's fault that your father betrayed Mary." He pointed to the woman in the picture. "Your mother, a dear friend of my wife, also died in the mill fire at the hands of two men. Not only Isaac Shaw, but your father too—my brother John Reeve."

Hope gasped in shock and confusion.

"We swore, as a community, to keep the truth from you—the truth that your father, with Isaac Shaw, was responsible for the death of two wonderful women: your mother, and my wife." Mr. Reeve lowered the picture and stared at Hope triumphantly, anger and bitterness flashing from his face in equal measure. "Your real name is Grace Reeve."

Hope spun away from his gloating face. It couldn't be true. If this was true, she was Edward Reeve's niece. It couldn't be true. He must be lying to her. He was mad. He was consumed with hate and bitterness. He was insane. She could not be his niece. She pushed past him and ran headlong to the stairs.

"And now the son manifests lunatic tendencies like his father," Mr. Reeve shouted behind her. The door to the bedroom slammed shut, and she could hear the triumph in his voice as he added, "Shaws have an almost mesmeric effect."

The echo of Hope's boots against the hallway flagstone pressed in around her. She ran to the front door but it was locked, and she as searched for a key she began to sob. To have seen her parents, no matter what it meant to Mr. Reeve, was an overwhelming relief. She wanted to go back upstairs and take the portrait, stare at the picture of her mother and father. The desire burned inside her with an almost overpowering passion. Then the awful awareness of her connection with Mr. Reeve washed over her again. More than anything she wanted to be rid of this infernal house and run away and never come back. Her father had betrayed her, just as Manny's father had betrayed him. Her body heaved with the crying, and slowly she slid to the floor. There was the sound of someone banging on the other side of the front door.

Mr. Reeve ran up behind Hope and knelt down. "I know you're shocked by this news, Grace. I am sorry that you have learned it all this way. I am consumed with regret that I have hidden the truth from you. You have not deserved to be betrayed like this."

One of the servants, a butler, came into the hallway. "Mr. Reeve, sir, the gentleman at the door . . ." The butler trailed off.

"Let me go. I want to go," Hope shouted. She could see the maid and another servant watching from a doorway.

"Leave this woman to me," Mr. Reeve said to the servants. "She's in distress. She'll be all right with some fresh air."

He grasped Hope's shoulders and dragged her across the hall to a large wooden chest. He lifted the lid and took out a pair of flintlock pistols. "Now hold still—do exactly as I say."

Fifteen

Consequence

You may wonder at the cause of John Reeve's delayed return to Ormley—why it was that he left his effort so long. An earlier return would have averted so much of the needless discomfort of the village. But the answer is simple. For the majority of years after the fire, he suffered from an unreliable recollection of the events. Unsure of his memories of the event, he believed himself guilty of some terrible crime, and so he stayed away. If this had not occurred, perhaps my story would have been very different. Yet this small fact was the sad stroke of misfortune that led to my being falsely accused. And John's forgetting what had happened was a great aid to Edward's plans.

Though my effort to rescue John had not been in vain, and though I had succeeded in keeping him alive, his knowledge of what had happened to him had vanished. Believing his brother Edward's testimony that he, John, was the guilty party, he ran away in fear of the gallows, and remained in hiding for some sixteen years—until a fortuitous meeting with a former servant to the Reeve family began to trigger new memories.

Nevertheless, there it was—my death, John's forgetting, his fear and subsequent exile. The opportunity for Edward's crime was presented. Given his secret compulsion to risk, complicated by a terrible grief and desire for revenge, the temptation to lie and thereby eliminate a debt and gain a fortune in the same simple stroke was simply too great to resist.

Immediately following John's rescue, he was found to be in a state of distraction and distress. To the rescuers' alarm, he was unable to provide explanation of what had happened inside the mill. He was attended to by a doctor from Northwood who declared him unsound, and in this unfortunate condition Hope's father was admitted to the lunatic asylum. I know of only one visit made by Edward to his brother during this period, though it must be said that the whole affair took only a week.

Edward went in order to assess for himself his brother's condition, with the understanding that he might take John into his own home. But this never transpired, and John, bequeathed with a small sum of money, subsequently disappeared.

A heron launched out of the water, flapping its way along the river. It beat past the mill, struggling against the wind, and headed into the woodland.

Manny saw a crowd of villagers loitering in the road outside Mr. Reeve's manor house. What were they doing? It must have gone wrong. Hope had been caught. Manny paused at the footbridge, trying to work out what to do. The voices from the crowd sounded angry, dangerous, agitated. It would not do to be afraid. He stepped forward.

As he stepped forward, he saw her. She stood, her hands clasped in front of her, with Reeve at her side. Reeve was smiling as he placated the restless villagers. Then Manny saw Will, angry and shouting, protesting about something.

Manny plunged through the crowd, struggling to reach the front, and before he knew it, he was standing isolated and all had become quiet. A hush descended, and he realized all of the villagers were watching him.

"Ah, Mr. Shaw," Mr. Reeve said contemptuously, seeming untroubled by Manny's sudden arrival. There was an awkward pause, as if people were supposed to have laughed at the ironic formal address. No one uttered a sound. "It is fortunate that you have decided to return—no doubt the authorities will look favorably on such a turn of heart."

Manny felt as though he had entered a dream. He looked around at the crowd, saw their perplexed expressions and knew his moment had come.

"I'm not a thief," he began, "but there is someone here who's guilty, a man who's hidden the truth from us." Manny said it without looking back at Reeve. He was determined to maintain a calmness, to include the crowd in his revelation of why he had returned. Manny watched their faces register his words. Only then did he turn back to face the mill owner. "I met an exiled man on the moors. Hope's father. He knows who you are, Reeve."

There was a gulping sob from Hope. Manny had expected the accusation to be greeted with a roar of outrage. But there was an eerie silence broken only by Hope's sobs. In confusion Manny turned back to the crowd. "Mr. Reeve hid the truth about Hope's father. The truth is that Mr. Reeve might have been guilty of killing his wife—it weren't me dad. I've found Hope's father. His name is John."

Trying to feel triumphant he glanced at Hope, but she wouldn't meet his eyes. She looked pale, as if she was at death's doorway.

"Let her go, Reeve," Manny suddenly shouted, striding up the steps toward the man, angry that Hope should be so needlessly humiliated. Manny took her hand but she did not respond, and Mr. Reeve pulled her back from him, smiling like a demon.

Dullness and then panic spread through Manny's chest. He understood neither Hope's behavior nor Mr. Reeve's confidence. He glanced back at Will and saw confusion and shame in his brother's face.

Then Hope began to step away, back toward the house.

"John Reeve was my brother," Mr. Reeve hissed, stepping between Hope and Manny. "He was guilty, just like your father. But we thought my niece deserved not to know about her shame. My sacrifice was to let her go. Our intention had been that she would grow up free from shame." He gestured to some of the men. "Take this thief and miscreant away, and someone fetch the constable."

Manny couldn't move. Hope was Reeve's niece? But how could that be true? He looked at her and knew she too believed the claim. Then, with awful certainty, he knew the claim was the truth.

He looked around and saw Will staring up at him, saw the crowd drawing closer. The world had just come crashing down, and Manny no longer knew what to do. The memories of his spiritual experiences now seemed hollow and meaningless. How could he have been so hasty to rush back into this village, with so little proof on his side? Had he taken leave of his senses?

He felt a tug at his arm. He could not resist arrest. It was over. They were dragging him away, back through the crowd. He had no desire to fight back. Hope was gone, and so was his future. Her silence said everything. He didn't have words to bring her back, and he dropped his gaze so that he did not have to look at the manor house. He had been a fool.

Suddenly there was a flurry of movement and some shouting. In the blur of his thoughts, Manny heard a familiar voice.

"No, leave him! It's a lie. Mr. Reeve hid it—the letter. Where is it?"

Manny realized with shock that it was Will who was shouting, Will who had rushed onto the steps and grabbed hold of Reeve, Will who was now trying to get past the mill owner and into the house. It looked like he might actually overpower him. "What have you done with it?"

Before anyone could stop him, Will had wrestled Mr. Reeve to the ground. Something fell from the mill owner's pocket, and then there was a bang—the sound of a single gunshot—and for a moment, total silence.

As the crowd surged forward, there was another gunshot. Then the door to Mr. Reeve's house slammed shut, barricading both the mill master and his newly declared niece from the villagers. The air was filled with the sound of Manny's mam screaming, men shouting.

Manny struggled loose from his captors and saw his mam pulling her hair, her face contorted by grief. He lost sight of her as the crowd gathered around a fallen body. Pushing through the melee of weavers, he saw Will lying on the ground. His brother was bleeding, hands covered in blood, his eyes wide. He was struggling to breathe. A bloody piece of paper was clutched in his fist.

Manny dropped down and grabbed him, terrified at the sight of his brother gasping for breath. All animosity had gone. Manny could barely speak.

Will struggled to look at him, and a faint glimmer of relief passed across his face. "Manny," he gasped. "I . . . went to see Mr. Alderman. I— wanted to say sorry." He gulped and then shivered.

Manny gripped his brother's shirt, suddenly panicking. Blood smeared his hands.

"Don't believe Reeve," Will said.

"What . . . what do you mean?"

"He's hiding . . ." Will said. The effort had cost him strength, and his grip grew weaker.

Manny stared at his brother in horror. Will was dying. "Where was Hope?" Manny demanded. He couldn't imagine why Reeve might have taken her.

"Manny . . ."

"Where was she?"

"She broke in."

Manny choked. "I know. But . . . you saw her. I don't understand."

"I tried to help her."

"What?"

"Manny. I never wanted Hope or you to leave . . ." Will was trying to sit up, but Manny could see the pain was too great. His brother's face was gray and covered with sweat. He was desperately trying to say something else. "I've paid, Manny. Two days ago." He was crying now, spluttering. "I . . . I were angry. I couldn't make you change. I argued with Mr. Alderman, and I pushed him. He fell—on the rocks. I didn't mean for him to get hurt . . ." Will's voice trailed off and he shook again.

Fear crept over Manny. He wanted to get Hope away from Mr. Reeve. But he couldn't leave Will. He tried to cradle his brother's limp body.

"Mr. Reeve were afraid I'd tell." Will stared up at him. "I went back to Reeve for the letter. He wanted to hide it. I wanted to stop him. I wanted to make up. I tried . . ." He gazed at Manny as if appealing for compassion and suddenly looked very vulnerable, very childlike. "Manny, I'm not ready to die."

The force of the words went straight to the center of Manny's soul. In spite of all the arguments and mistakes, he was of the same flesh and blood; they were brothers. "This isn't your fault, Will. Not yours. Do you hear me?" Manny stared at him and then closed his eyes, praying with all his might. Will couldn't die. He was too young. He'd been wrong but he wasn't evil.

"Forgive me," Manny whispered.

His brother smiled weakly.

Manny looked around, desperate for a way to prevent the inevitable. He could see his mam held up by a knot of weavers. He struggled out of his coat and bundled it up into a pillow.

Will's grip tightened on Manny's hand again. "Hope loves you. I was always jealous." He turned his face to the moorland and seemed to gain a little more confidence. "I got the letter back." His grip on it weakened as he offered it up to Manny. "Look after our mam." There was a last smile and then a long, rattling breath.

Manny leaned over him. He shook his brother gently and then more desperately. "Will! No . . . Will!"

But there was no response. In that moment, and now that it was no longer possible to tell him, Manny realized how much he had loved his brother. Despite the arguments, the fights, the jealousy over Hope, the rivalry and all of the petty ridiculous resentment, Manny knew he had always loved him. He longed to be able to call him back, to give him life. He felt the stab of grief this death would bring to his mam.

He gently pulled the letter from Will's grasp, then let go of his brother's body and fell back as two men from the crowd pushed past him. They knelt down, closed Will's eyes, and then lifted the body and carried it away. Manny stared around in anger and held up the blooded letter. "Do you hear me?" he screamed. "This weren't his fault." He tried to stand, but the ground was spinning and he fell. He lay stretched out on the dirt, weeping, breathing the dust, feeling the stone bruising his ribs. He grieved for his choice to run away from the mill, grieved the choice to run to the moors, cursed himself for losing the letter. And he wept because of the kind of death his brother had seen and the distress that had been brought upon Hope.

Manny barely cared about looking at the letter. This whole affair was Mr. Reeve's fault. He had lied to everyone. And even now he'd managed to escape. Manny clutched at the stones on the highway. Then he stumbled up and flung them at the manor house, smashing one of the windows. The crowd closed around him, their hands pulling at his shirt. One of the villagers grabbed him by the shoulder, and then Manny felt the hand yanked away. Another man pushed him to the ground and tried to hold him there, but Manny twisted loose. The air was filled with bodies, pushing and falling around him. Then there was shouting and the sound of more splintering glass. He crawled away.

The Orm had risen because of all the recent rain. Manny stood by the edge of the river, listening to the thrash of the water. His hands were still covered with Will's blood, and he crouched to wash them clean. He felt cold and alone. It was too hard to believe his brother was dead.

One of the weavers stepped down the embankment to join him.

"Hope'll be afraid," Manny said vacantly. He saw other villagers watching from the road. A few weavers had gathered around the bridge. Suddenly he realized he couldn't see his mam. She must hate him now.

"We're just standing here," he said. He knew he should be doing something, but he couldn't think straight. His mind was empty, as if dislocated from the rest of his body.

The weaver looked awkward and shifted his weight from one foot to the other. He squinted back, putting his hands into his pockets. The lines on his face became furrows. Manny suddenly wanted to scream at him, to demand answers, to understand why no one had ever asked questions of Mr. Reeve before.

The man stepped nearer. "It doesn't mean she's going to be hurt."

"Don't—don't come any closer." In spite of his efforts to change, in spite of his determination, Manny knew he had never truly been humble. He picked a stone out of the mud. It was smooth and cold, almost as round as a musket ball. He hurled it into the river. "Why did it have to be this way?" he whispered.

The man cleared his throat. "Listen, lad, they've sent word to the constables in Northwood. We reckon as Reeve is hiding somewhere on 'is estate. The police'll watch all the roads for sight of him, though, in case he escapes."

"But we should be looking for him as well," Manny said. He struggled up the embankment. "They're probably still close."

"No, lad, he's armed. The police'll catch him."

Rage burst out of Manny before he could do anything to stop it, and he struggled up the river bank, clutching at stones, then ran full tilt toward the mill. "He's a liar! He killed my brother, and my father, too."

A mill window smashed, splintering glass into the courtyard. Manny picked up another stone and looked around, hardly caring what or whom he saw. But the villagers had clearly been incited by the actions of Mr. Reeve as well, and they surged into the mill yard behind him. Another window spat glass over the flagstones. Men ran everywhere, shouting madly.

Manny turned back toward Mr. Reeve's house. He began to push through the weavers, to get through the gates at the mill. Then on the highway he saw a woman, and as though called back from a distant world he recognized Sister Aitkin. She stood alone, near the bridge, obviously afraid of the rioting but refusing to turn back. The sight of her made Manny regain some control. "How did you know to come here?" he said, running to her.

"Because you didn't come back," she said. "I couldn't find the solicitor. I sent word to Elder Armitage." She was looking round open-mouthed at the scenes of complete disorder. "What's happened?"

"Hope's gone. Me brother's dead."

Manny stared at the bloodied letter and then held it toward Sister Aitkin.

A shrill whistle split the air.

A single, determined-looking constable,
with truncheon drawn, scythed through the
rioting villagers, his face crimson and his
hat askew. The men scattered.

"Any more of this here disturbance," the policeman bellowed, jabbing the truncheon furiously toward the rapidly quieting crowd, "and I'll have the lot of you arrested before you can say jackrabbit."

He strode over to Manny, seized him roughly, and slapped handcuffs on his wrists. Manny began to protest and held up the bloodstained letter, but somehow his heart wasn't in the fight anymore. All he could see was a dying brother and a confusing vision of Hope. He'd failed, and the worst of it was that he couldn't find it in his heart to keep trying.

"Not a word, young fella me lad," the policeman said. "You've already caused enough trouble." He took the letter and gingerly folded it before placing it in one of his pockets. Then, gripping Manny's collar, he spoke to the crowd. "And I'll be after any of the rest of you who care to make trouble. There'll be more of us on the way."

Sister Aitkin had vanished, and the crowd of villagers looked restless, as if the initial shock and intimidation of the constable's arrival was wearing off. Trouble brewed again. One of the weavers picked up a stone and stepped out from the crowd, his arm moving back as if he meant to throw the stone. But the policeman saw him and pointed the truncheon at him. The crowd moved back, and without another word the constable turned away and steered Manny back toward the highway to Northwood.

Sixteen

Obadiah Thomas

Still struggling to comprehend what had transpired in Ormley, Manny was only vaguely conscious that the constable had, with considerable effort, been trying to read the letter. He'd looked at it all the way to Northwood, so either he didn't read well or had insisted on attempting to march and read at the same time. In any case, the contents of the letter appeared to have affected his opinion of the whole affair. By the time they reached the outskirts of town, the constable was no longer hauling but guiding.

Expecting to be taken straight to the police station, Manny was surprised when the policeman led him straight past it and escorted him along Main Street until they reached a small alley called New Court. He then proceeded to remove the handcuffs, telling Manny he was no longer suspected of committing a crime.

It caught some attention, the large and awkward constable removing handcuffs from Manny's wrists. Several passersby stopped a short distance away, no doubt speculating over the cause of this unlikely event.

The officer gave the letter to Manny and smiled in a sort of gruffly compassionate way. "I believe you'll know what to do with this, young lad. The man you'll need is down there." He pointed to a nearby doorway on New Court. Then, preempting Manny's question, he added, "It's not just the letter, lad. It's the combination of circumstantial evidence. Don't concern yourself—I'll come and find you at the solicitor's." After giving a courteous nod, the constable turned and strode back up Main Street toward the police station.

Manny stood a while, trying to collect his thoughts and make sense of the last few hours. He felt stuck in a dream from which he longed to awake, and yet here he was, free and approved of by the constable, now with the law on his side and escorted to the very man he had been counseled to find all along.

Manny looked down at the envelope. It would no longer matter if he read the letter before giving it to the solicitor.

But the letter was incomplete. It simply read:

My dear Hope,

I wish you to know of my great happiness at the event of your baptism into the Church of the Latter-day Saints. I know more of this church than you may imagine, and I see the hand of God in your conversion to this faith. I want to tell you also of my great joy at your desire to be married to young Manny Shaw. He has not been able to quite tell me as much, but I can see the looming question approaching, and your marriage will have my blessing. In spite of what you may have imagined, I do not care what others will think. The reasons for this will, I hope, become clearer over the next few days. I have arranged to give Manny a sum of money which I hope should enable you to begin your preparations.

Hope, there is a pressing matter which I now address with shame and deep regret. I pray you will forgive my secrecy with regards to your past. I am ashamed even now to think that I have misled you with such deliberation. Nevertheless, you must know of my intent to do what I believed to be correct

Manny tried to imagine what else Mr. Alderman could have written. It felt wrong to accept that Hope was truly Mr. Reeve's niece, yet even this single page seemed to imply that Mr. Alderman believed it. Did this mean the farmer had also been involved in the conspiracy of silence? There could be no other explanation. Why had it been undertaken with such care? Why was Hope prevented from knowing about her parentage? Surely Edward Reeve could have taken her in himself.

An alarming and uncomfortable answer began to suggest itself. Was it possible that John Reeve was guilty of the crime, as his brother Edward Reeve claimed—that hiding John's identity and Hope's was one means of protecting her from the shame Will and Manny and their mam had lived with? Was this an elaborate attempt to cheat the village and protect the interests of the entire Reeve family?

A small sign, extending from the wall on Manny's left, creaked in a gust of wind. On the board was written, in plain gold type, *Obadiah Thomas, Solicitor.*

The voices on Main Street behind Manny merged with the sounds of carts and stagecoaches. Even though he had not spoken to Hope for over two days, he had always been aware of her, close to her in purpose. He now felt completely bereft of her companionship— truly separated from her for the first time since they'd parted.

What he longed for was some kind of assurance that his vision of his father was not just the longings of a desperate mind. He yearned for some guiding principle to see him through this returning heartache, one last reserve of courage and faith.

A constant stream of people hurried along Main Street, past the turn onto New Court, holding their hats and shawls against the wind. Those who had been curious about the odd behavior of the constable had now gone, and everyone else seemed oblivious to Manny's presence.

He swallowed, nervous not so much about what lay immediately ahead but of the frailty of his mind. He kept seeing Will in his head, kept thinking about Mr. Reeve and Hope. Manny's earlier resolution to go back to Ormley seemed embarrassingly naïve now, and it almost seemed pointless to take this letter to Mr. Thomas. Manny wanted to believe John's claim, but how could he dispute Edward Reeve's story? Indeed, John had seemed reluctant to reveal his full name. But that didn't mean he was guilty—or did it?

The sign creaked again, almost as if it was calling to Manny. Looking up, he saw that the solicitor's office was dark, although he could just make out the shape of a man sitting at a desk. Gritting his teeth, Manny climbed the three steps to the door. The doorbell pinged as he entered the office. He stepped inside and leaned back against the door to shut it. The noise from Main Street dulled. The room felt warm; it smelled of the coal fire burning gently in the grate. It was as though he had walked into another time where there was only order and peace. He stood for a few seconds, basking in the quiet steadiness.

A man with a pale face and mournful eyes looked up from a desk at the back of the room. He put down his quill and looked at his work. Then he pushed his seat back and stood, breaking the silence. "Can I help you?"

Manny held onto the door handle. "Mr. Thomas?"

"No."

Manny felt deflated. "I need to speak with him." He glanced back out the window. It was difficult to sustain his resolve when all he could hear were Will's last words. "Can you tell me when he'll be back?"

"I expect him shortly."

"Then I'll wait." Manny forced a smile and pointed to the bookshop on the other side of the street. "I won't be far away." He turned to leave.

"Is he expecting you?" the clerk asked.

"No."

The man looked at his desk and sat down. "He may not be able to see you straight away. He's very busy just now." He started writing again.

"I must speak with him."

The clerk nodded.

———

Manny stared out from behind the grimy window of the bookshop, praying Hope would be safe. He tried to reassure himself that the police were now on his side and would soon be able to arrest Edward Reeve for Will's murder. The memory of holding his dying brother came forcibly into Manny's mind again. It was too much to believe he was gone. He could still feel the weight of Will's limp body, still hear the long rattle of his final breath. It couldn't be true that he was dead. But it was. Manny thought he ought to feel more than just shock—that he ought to feel more grief.

He absentmindedly picked up a copy of *The Diary of Samuel Pepys* and tried to be still, hoping he would not need to wait too long for Mr. Thomas to return. But he opened the book to the account of the fire of London and closed it quickly. He suddenly wanted to run back to Ormley and search for Hope.

An old woman was peering at him from the other side of the glass. For a split second he thought it was his mam, and with that thought another thought flashed into his mind. He was a young man, smarting from Mr. Reeve's whipping, his mam crying into her hands, tears running down her weary face. "The fire should never have happened, Manny. Mr. Reeve could have been ruined. He requires us not to speak of the past. You mustn't anger him. I can't afford for you or William to lose your job. You have to learn to forget the fire. And you must always keep Dad's crime to yourself, always a secret. It was his crime, not ours. Silence is the price of redeeming our name."

The memory was broken by the sound of laughter. Manny looked up. The old woman had gone, and instead he saw two men—one wiry, the other a shorter, bearded man, standing just outside the open door to the bookshop.

"Well, it was fortunate timing," the wiry man said, smiling. He stood at the bottom of the steps and pulled out a set of keys, then returned them to his pocket, shaking his head. "I've hardly had time to stop since I arrived back from Manchester." He climbed the steps and opened the door to the office. "It's nothing but work, work, and more work."

"Then I'm glad I saw you when I did," said the bearded man. "I'll look forward to relieving the debt."

"Excuse me," Manny said a few minutes later. He stood just inside the solicitor's office, as he had done before.

The clerk looked up from the back of the room. "This is the gentlemen, sir."

Mr. Thomas removed a pair of reading glasses. "Indeed." He smiled and pointed to a chair in front of his desk. "Please, have a seat."

Manny felt a sudden wave of apprehension. Having grown up in an environment of concealment, the invitation to make a disclosure was deeply disconcerting.

The solicitor must have noticed Manny's discomfort. "Come and speak with me in confidence."

The clerk looked slighted. "Is there anything you'd like me to do, sir?"

"No, thank you, Braithwaite." Mr. Thomas said it graciously but pointedly, and then gestured for Manny to follow him into a room at the side of the office.

Inside this second room, Manny sat down, a little more at ease but still conscious of the imminent responsibility of explaining, of trying to make some sense of the chaos in Ormley.

A line of portraits hung behind the solicitor's desk—paintings, he assumed, of lawyers, all of them resembling Mr. Thomas. He felt as if he had suddenly been brought before an inquiry, that he was standing in the dock. On the desk was a bottle of ink with a quill pen and a few loose sheaves of paper. Manny kept silent and watched as Mr. Thomas closed the door and walked across to his desk. He sat down and shuffled the papers into a neat pile. Sunlight pooled on the veneer of the desk. Manny squinted and looked away from the glare. Mr. Thomas put his papers down and leaned forward, his hands clasped. "Now, tell me why you are here." He said it politely, but there was a hint of impatience in his voice.

"I . . ." How was Manny to sit here and calmly discuss the wrenching bereavements and crimes he had just witnessed? His mind felt clear, yet chaotic at the same time.

Mr. Thomas's eyes seemed to flicker with a more sincere curiosity. "What's your name?"

"Manny—Ephraim Immanuel Shaw. I—someone . . . my brother's been murdered, and someone else has been kidnapped."

Suddenly he had the solicitor's complete attention, and the words came pouring out. "It's Mr. Reeve—the mill owner at Ormley. There were a letter . . . it had a message for Hope Alderman, from her guardian, Mr. George Alderman. I think the letter is about Hope's real father. But I found him me'self—he's been arrested. I know that Mr. Reeve won't let Hope find out. He shot me brother. We weren't speaking to one another but . . . I . . . Hope Alderman, she—"

"You're Isaac Shaw's son aren't you?" The solicitor asked it gently.

Manny hesitated. "I'm the son of an alleged criminal," he said. "I'm in love wi' a girl whose Dad was— I didn't know. I don't know what I think any more. I thought I knew but . . . Mr. Reeve's looked after me family since me Dad died.

I don't . . . I can't carry the weight . . ." Manny felt exhausted and he sat, listening to the muffled cries of the traders shouting, far away on Main Street, and then to the footsteps on the other side of the door.

Mr. Thomas waited.

"I've been hiding," explained Manny at last. "The police thought I'd stolen some money. I weren't guilty, though. Mr. Alderman gave it to me." He held up the letter as proof. "The money were for me and Hope to get married."

The light from window dimmed.

Mr. Thomas stared at him. "Mr. Shaw." His voice had become compassionate, kindly.

Manny looked up, confused.

"Tell me what you know about Edward Reeve's family."

"I don't . . . I can't . . ." Manny went silent. He could feel the bruise of the rope, smell the room where he was punished.

"Mr. Shaw."

Manny looked up. "But what about Hope?"

The solicitor was leaning forward, closer, as if to urge him to speak. "You must talk about what happened."

Manny felt desperate. Pain stabbed through the side of his face. "I don't understand."

"Don't you?"

"No. I found Hope's real father, but he didn't tell me who he was—" Manny longed to be able to leave, to hide from the confusion and pain. "I wanted to help Hope . . . we needed to help Hope."

"But you are," replied Mr. Thomas. "You say you think your father was falsely accused. Now, who else died in the fire?"

"I can't . . . I . . ."

"It was a woman."

"Yes," Manny whispered. He knew the woman's identity, although he didn't understand how. He was thinking of the fire, trying desperately to work everything out.

"It was Hope Alderman's mother," Mr. Thomas said. "Edward Reeve's sister-in-law."

There was a knock at the door and Braithwaite peered in. "Excuse me, sir. I thought you might want to know that Constable Davidson and John Reeve have arrived. And" —he cleared his throat— "I just received this." He held up a note. "It was delivered from Ormley. I believe it concerns the young man here."

Seventeen

An Everlasting Truth

Manny kept looking at John, wondering if his fears about the fire could be correct. The withdrawn and darkened face did little to alleviate his suspicion. But he waited, hoping against hope that something would be said to put his mind at rest. He wondered if the note had news of Hope, but Mr. Thomas was saying nothing, only looking grieved.

Then, as if no longer deliberating over what was to be done, the solicitor seemed to come to himself. He glanced up at Constable Davidson and John Reeve, then pushed the original bloodstained letter back toward Manny.

"You're officially deemed innocent of the charge of theft, Mr. Shaw. However, I'm sorry to have to tell you that . . ." He picked up the note Braithwaite had brought in.

"It's about Hope, isn't it?" Manny interrupted. He felt a great weight settle in the pit of his stomach. The note had bad news.

The solicitor removed his spectacles and rubbed his eyes. He looked tired. "No, it's not about Miss Alderman," he said gently. "It's a letter from Edward Reeve about your mother. Apparently, she's left Ormley with him."

The two men behind Manny began to murmur. Manny thought he might be going insane. His mam was with Edward Reeve? Had she decided to go away with him, or been forced to? The room spun around Manny. He took a deep breath, trying to restore his bearing and prevent himself from falling over. He realized John Reeve was holding him by the arm and that Mr. Thomas was speaking again. Meanwhile, Braithwaite had excused himself, but the door had been left ajar. Clearly, he was just as intrigued by the note as everyone else.

"There is no word on Hope's whereabouts," Mr. Thomas said apologetically.

Manny stood. He needed some air. "I can't stay here—I must be allowed to go. Please, I . . ."

The solicitor gestured for him to sit again. "I'm afraid I must burden you further, Mr. Shaw, though I had hoped to be able to set your mind to rest. I'm sorry for what more you must try to reconcile. I fear that it will not be easy to bear, especially in these new circumstances." He held up the note and passed it to Constable Davidson. "Mr. Reeve wishes for you to be informed of the truth. There is here a confession of sorts."

John Reeve started to protest. "Mr. Thomas, I hardly think this is the time to be . . . my daughter, Manny's mother . . ."

But the solicitor continued. "I believe, Mr. Shaw, that you have been one of the many victims of a serious fraud."

"I . . ." began Manny, but he couldn't think of anything to say. It seemed peculiar to be discussing this when all he could think of was his mam and Hope.

"This morning I was called to the police station. There I met this man." Mr. Thomas gestured toward Hope's father. "John Reeve. He can tell you what he told me."

"He needs to know, yes," John said, "but I want the constabulary alerted. They must be informed about this message. I do not trust its reliability. We require assistance—my brother is liable to do almost anything."

Constable Davidson puffed out his chest, importantly waving the note. "I'll keep hold of this, sir, if I might. I shall certainly inform my superiors, Mr. Reeve, and we shall devise a plan of action."

Mr. Thomas nodded his agreement, after which the police constable left. Then the solicitor turned to face John Reeve. "I assure you I am deeply concerned about the welfare of your daughter." He trailed off here, as if conscious of the implications for Manny. "But I think it only fair to present your testimony. You can see what state this has left the young man in. He must be allowed to hear what you have to say." Then Mr. Thomas added pointedly, "It will give him some understanding, an asset he is in severe need of."

John looked torn between conflicting loyalties. "The Ormley Mill fire happened in the wake of several people's desire to become Latter-day Saints—Mormons," he began eventually. "And your father was one of them."

Manny was aware of this interest in the Mormons, but he still wasn't sure if he could trust John. The news that his mother had gone away with Mr. Reeve threatened to overwhelm him entirely. He couldn't make any sense of it. Knowing Hope might be in danger worried him as well. Where was she?

"How is it possible that I've never known any of this?" Manny said quietly. "I've lived in Ormley all me life. Why did the villagers hide the truth about Hope? No one ever said anything about me dad, either. Me mam" —he felt a pang of anxiety upon thinking about her— "let slip about me dad's interest in the religion a day or two back, but she wouldn't say no more of it. But Mr. Alderman or anyone could have said . . ." It seemed incredible that such a secret could have been kept for all this time. Manny turned suddenly on John. "If you were innocent, why did it take you so long to come back?"

John began to explain what had happened to his memory, of the visit Edward made to the asylum, and of John's own decision to go into exile. "I was a coward," he said finally. "I made a mistake in not coming back . . . the fear took hold of me. Before my memory of what happened fully returned, I believed I was indeed a criminal, and I wished only to stay out of the country. So I wrote to George to ask him to swear not to tell Hope."

"So, knowledge of this interest in the Mormons was kept secret before and after the fire," Mr.

Thomas interjected. "Can you confirm this, Mr. Shaw?"

"Yes," Manny said dazedly. "I mean no. Like I said before, me mam let it slip a couple of days ago that me Dad had been interested."

"Why didn't you ever ask anyone about your father's death?"

Manny tried to focus, but there was so much information swimming around in his head. "What?"

"Why didn't you ever ask about your father's death?"

"I did . . . once."

"And what happened?"

"Mr. Reeve beat me."

"Did he say anything to you?"

"He said asking about the fire were wrong. That it would upset me mam. That talking about Dad would cause her more shame than she deserved. That she were a good woman. And that I should keep her dignity by keeping silent."

"Did she know you'd been beaten?"

"Yes."

"And?"

"She told me to keep quiet. She's afraid of the workhouse. Me mam's always said she'd die there if Will or me lost our jobs. She said I weren't to speak about the past. That we had always to show Mr. Reeve our thanks for his compassion to us."

Mr. Thomas nodded. "Thank you." He smiled, pausing as if eager to speak and yet not quite sure how to continue. "The fire, of course, was blamed on your father and John."

"But it wasn't our fault," John said firmly. "I believe the fire was intended to discredit your father, and that it was exploited to protect my brother's fortune. Of course, his gambling was safeguarded, a useful diversion from his grief."

For a few moments, Manny wondered if he should have felt something more than relief. But his shame was no longer required—it had never been required. Perhaps he should be angry, outraged even. Yet he could feel none of this, even when he tried. Just numb relief.

Suddenly, unexpectedly, he thought of his vision on the moors, of his father's face, of the calmness and the love he'd felt. There was life beyond death. There was more to his life than this suffering, this constant struggle for peace. There was a reason to keep faith in his future. The thought comforted Manny, beginning to relieve his confusion. And, briefly, it helped to ease the shock of Will's passing. Manny knew he'd seen his father, that it was no figment of an anxious mind.

He laughed a little and stood up shakily. "I think me dad's been guiding me." He turned to face Hope's father. "But you were in the mill when the fire started."

"I know." John's voice was calm now, more measured. He gazed at Manny as if the declaration of his father's involvement had struck some chord. "We feared for the villagers' jobs. They were threatened with losing their employment after Edward confessed to his possible bankruptcy, a fruit of his inability to stay away from gambling.

During the meeting, there was an argument, an accident, and the mill caught fire."

"But you said you lost your memory—how did you remember what happened?"

"For some years now, I've been at sea. On a recent voyage to India I happened upon a man who was once one of my family's servants. He recognized me and we spoke. My ship was in port for a number of days, and as we conversed, I began to piece together facts that had been blurred by the confusion I felt after the fire.

"Before my brother came to England from India, he'd managed to acquire a large sum of money on credit, a figure in the region of fifty thousand pounds."

Manny looked up, startled at the amount.

John paused, acknowledging the surprise, and then, after a moment of silence, he continued. "This he managed to do by finding a wealthy family with an eligible daughter. Miss Ellen McCarthy. He married her and they came back to England, to Lancashire, where they built a cotton mill close to his estate.

"Then the Mormons arrived. And it wasn't just your father and I who expressed interest. Ellen was also intrigued, and Edward became jealous, afraid of this call to change. I think, in fact, that he simply doubted his capacity to convert. It was at this time I discovered his compulsion to gambling.

"At the same time, the mill was failing. Edward panicked. The mill was failing, and, so it seems, was my brother's marriage. He and I became embittered over his gambling. Edward argued that he was justified by the intent to try to provide for Ellen. He'd persuaded himself that he was trying to secure his wife's future."

"I don't see how this—"

"The crime Edward is charged with arises from this history of credit," John explained patiently, "because this former servant said he learned that my brother's debt had been cancelled out of compassion, in the belief that the fire was started deliberately by two of the mill's weavers. I knew then it was your father and me that he had accused. Edward had persuaded me to leave the country, pretending he was helping me to escape from the charge of a heinous crime, when all along he knew I wasn't guilty. I also believe Ellen may have been expecting their first child when she died. Guilt and grief have destroyed my brother.

"In any case he seized his chance to defraud his creditors, cover up the truth of his misdeed, and secure a way to hide his love of gambling—all at the cost of a simple lie."

Manny walked across to the window, still wondering about his mam and Hope. "But how did the fire actually start?" he asked.

"We don't know. Possibly an oil lamp. During the meeting, I left the room in anger at my brother's stubbornness. When I'd calmed down I returned and heard Edward shouting at Ellen. Then there was a sound like a breaking lamp. Edward panicked. We thought he was going to get help—he ran without helping anyone, not even his wife. I think he might have tried to come back, but the fire and all it implied made him insensible. The fire spread so quickly that the women and I became trapped. Your father managed to escape—he was desperate to raise help from the village, but by the time he returned Ellen was dead. And so was my wife."

"So . . . you and me dad had nothing to do wi' actually starting the fire?"

"Not the fire, no. But we were there—we'd called the meeting. Perhaps my brother convinced himself we were responsible for it."

"But . . ."

John shrugged as if acknowledging the awfulness of it all, and Mr. Thomas took up the conversation.

"Since the events of this morning, the police shall have no difficulty in arresting Edward Reeve. But until this morning, well, you know that people believed his testimony. There was no one to dispute it. It was one man's word against another. And Edward didn't run away. You know that people always assumed it was John and your father who were to blame."

Suddenly Manny was angry. The room seemed to pull away and then race back. His family's life had been woven with secrets, injustice, and suffering. All at the hands of a lunatic who cared only for himself and whose selfishness was killing the village. Manny's head and heart felt strangely disconnected. Mr. Reeve's charity was a lie. The man was a hypocrite. He was to blame for all the suffering—every single miserable day of it.

Manny clenched his teeth and closed his eyes. He must not give in to his anger, but it was so powerful, so consuming. All he could see was Will's lifeless eyes, and the fact that Hope was at the mercy of a reckless killer. As for what his mam was thinking, Manny had no idea. The anger threatened to drive him mad. He wanted to fight, and he almost didn't care whom. He felt himself slowly succumbing to the temptation to such rage as he had never known before. The appeal of it was overwhelming, for revenge would be justice. And yet he knew it would not.

With great effort, Manny brought himself back to his original purpose. He opened his eyes and realized Mr. Thomas was speaking to him again. "Remember, Mr. Shaw, Mr. Reeve held his pregnant wife dead in his arms. They'd been married only a few years. His life was shattered by this bereavement."

The words washed over Manny like a douse of cold water, and for the first time he began to comprehend what the anger could do to him. It could make him become like Mr. Reeve.

Manny recoiled. He could hardly believe that after all of the effort to get away from his grief he was now in danger of becoming exactly the same as the man he had most wished to leave behind. "How can I be free of this anger?" he whispered.

Mr. Thomas looked hesitant and then bent down and opened a drawer in his desk. "If you'd forgive my presumption to give advice, I should like to offer the only solution I know." He pulled out an old, worn Bible. "I'm not as devout as I might be, and I understand that you might be offended by my counsel. It may seem insensitive to say so at

214

this particular moment, but you must hold on to a trust in Christ, despite your shock."

"But how can I do that?" Manny asked meekly.

Mr. Thomas thumbed through the pages, then stopped and held the Bible open. He looked at Manny. "Perhaps these verses from Isaiah may be of some solace. 'He was despised and rejected of men; a man of sorrows, and acquainted with grief: and we hid as it were our faces from him; he was despised, and we esteemed him not. Surely he hath borne our griefs, and carried our sorrows: yet we did esteem him stricken, smitten of God, and afflicted. But he was wounded for our transgressions, he was bruised for our iniquities: the chastisement of our peace was upon him; and with his stripes we are healed.'"

"But what about Mr. Reeve?" Manny said, wanting to accept the counsel. 'What about me mam, and Hope?"

"Try not to be afraid. You are no longer alone. Let the law take its course. You can receive the strength to be at peace."

Mr. Thomas smiled at him, an encouraging kind of smile, and pointed to the Bible again. "However much you feel you cannot do this, the Lord has shown us the way to escape from the bondage of fear and hate: 'And whosoever shall compel thee to go a mile, go with him twain. . . . Love your enemies, bless them that curse you, do good to them that hate you, and pray for them which despitefully use you, and persecute you; That ye may be the children of your Father which is in heaven.'" The solicitor put the Bible down. "I know that seems a tall order, insensitive even, but it's the only way to be at peace."

Manny closed his eyes and nodded. But he wasn't sure he could be like that.

"The police will apprehend Edward Reeve," Mr. Thomas said confidently. "They'll bring him into the police station for questioning. If there's any need, I can act as advocate to John, Hope, and yourself. In the circumstances, I'm quite sure the police will dismiss all charges against the three of you."

Manny opened his eyes and looked out at the darkening street. Rain began to fall. A young couple ran to take shelter in the entrance of the bookshop. They hunched close to each other in the doorway, laughing. The man peered up at the sky and the woman pulled him back. Then Manny thought he saw a younger, familiar-looking woman standing in the middle of the street. It couldn't be! But he was sure he had seen her: Hope, bedraggled in the rain and yet beautiful as ever. Then the rain fell more heavily, blurring the window. But it was her, it was Hope.

He ran to the door, suddenly elated, snatched from the despair he had been laboring under. Then he remembered something and felt quite reckless— he must make the request he'd meant to ask of Mr. Alderman three days ago. "Mr. Reeve, John, sir—can I ask for your blessing on a marriage?"

John Reeve looked surprised and then offended, as if he found the timing of Manny's request in bad taste.

Manny's voice raced now, keeping time with his pounding heart. "One day soon, me and Hope'll leave Ormley, like we wanted. We'll get married as we planned." He was surprised at how renewed he felt. "Me dad did come back. He said he would. I tell you, there's life beyond death. It's him 'as made all this happen—me dad, and perhaps Hope's mam as well."

Manny reached for the door handle.

A knock sounded at the other side of the door, after which Braithwaite peered in and said, "Excuse me, sir." He had a distinct look of triumph on his face, as if he finally felt joined to the drama unfolding around him. "There's a young lady here. She won't give her name. She's quite agitated. She's insisting that she must be allowed to see Ephraim Shaw and is asking to see her father—Mr. John Reeve."

Eighteen

My Weakness

Just as John was not without mistakes in the Ormley Mill affair, I confess that I too made a serious error of judgment that played a part in the circumstances of the fire. It was, as I came to see much later, a less tangible mistake than John's struggle to return to Ormley. But it was a weakness on my part that created part of the resentment. I had offended a man so much that the former friend had become an enemy. Now, just as the Bible made clear, the last farthing payment was being extracted.

I was not guilty of starting the fire, but of greed that impelled me to seek to remain on good terms with the Reeves. I had privately schemed for a share in their wealth. My greed also blinded me to the fact that I owed my employer an apology, one I was never able to extend. I failed to resolve my conflict, and my lack of humility led to the far-reaching consequences you have now been a witness to.

I confess I was ambitious—secretly I was wildly so. I was flattered by the Reeves' attention; they were kindly disposed to my wife and me, and I could see that by working hard and proving loyal to them I might profit thereby. I began to dream of being richer than I was. They were wealthy; I was envious. When I suggested that Edward become godfather to my children, my true motive was the fortune I might inherit by being related. When I learned of his dire financial situation I confess I felt disconsolate, not only for the well-being of the village but also because I believed the plans for my security could not be achieved. I am ashamed to admit to this calculating and underhand scheme. I was ashamed even then, though I persuaded myself that my desire for wealth was a noble one—that I was considering the future of my children.

I saw my life differently when I met the Mormon elders. They presented a different vision of prosperity, and I began to replace my greed with the appropriate desire for spiritual wealth. Yet Edward was genuinely affronted when he understood what it was I had tried to contrive for my family. The quest for an inappropriate share of another man's wealth was my undoing. I have paid dearly for it.

In the wake of the fire, I came to see how desperate Edward had been for genuine support—that my brief display of selfish endeavor had betrayed him. I had fractured the trust he held me in, and his anger twisted his mind until he came to truly believe I was responsible, with his brother, for the tragic circumstances of 1837. Edward could not come to forgive me, or anyone else for their part in the event.

I have been left to mourn the sad truth of the words of Jesus to his followers on the Sermon on the Mount: "Agree with thine adversary quickly, whiles thou art in the way with him; lest at any time the adversary deliver thee to the judge, and the judge deliver thee to the officer, and thou be cast into prison. Verily I say unto thee, Thou shalt by no means come out thence, till thou hast paid the uttermost farthing."

This payment for my slip—my moment of greed— has come to be exacted on my family in my absence. And thus you see the ultimate cause of my return to Ormley since my death.

Edward Reeve's capacity to acknowledge his blame was almost entirely lost. The distortion of his mind was the result. And, obsessed with keeping control over his crime, he was trapped. Oddly enough, I think the forced exposure brought by John's return might have come as a great relief. Yet there was also the greatest need for strength, and in this forced confessing, an increasing madness. I imagined Manny was becoming Reeve's object for revenge. I believed there would be nothing he wanted less than for my son to marry his niece—that he would see to it that Hope was taken from him. But none of us had reckoned on Lucy's strength or on the depth of her love for her family.

Away on Edward Reeve's estate, hidden within a thicket of trees, Lucy lay bound and gagged, and though I imagined she must feel terrified, she looked somehow serene, unafraid of the jeopardy she was in.

Reeve had sat for a long time in the quiet woods, staring out over the moors, apparently contemplating his escape. After struggling for several minutes to loosen her gag, Lucy had given up and lain still. But it was incomprehensible that she should be here now like this. I couldn't help gazing on her face—it was the picture of peace, and there was no sign of fear or anger. I didn't know whether it would prove useful for me to speak as I had to Manny, but there was nothing else I could think to do.

"Edward, I'm sorry."

But my voice was unheard; my attempt to apologize to him useless.

So, instead, I tried to comfort my wife. Accepting the situation we found ourselves in was all we could do. I am not sure when I first began to know it, but it was here, in this spirit of willing submission, that I began to feel the love of another presence—to feel the strength of the Lord's love. This all-healing force was what strengthened Lucy and me. To my surprise I saw that her gag had loosened and that she seemed more comfortable. She moved her feet, trying to huddle up and keep warm. I looked around, trying to see what Edward was doing. It was impossible to predict what he might do, but instinct told me that Lucy's life was in danger.

Edward stood statuesquely in front of the carriage, looking back in the direction of Ormley and seeming even more agitated than before. In his hands he held one of the pistols, and he kept turning it over and over, a man seeking to persuade himself to do something final. Then as Lucy watched, he suddenly stopped; clearly he had come to a decision. He stepped close to the horses and rubbed and patted their necks, talking just low enough that it would have been difficult for Lucy to hear.

"I need to keep away from them," he said. "I need to find somewhere to hide. Perhaps we should go back to India, maybe . . ." His voice trailed away. He squinted up at the storm clouds and then glanced back toward Ormley. Large spots of rain began to fall in the clearing. "I just need to get to the turnpike," he said to the horses, "and we'll make it. I'm sure of it."

Lucy wasn't well enough to manage as a hostage. I wondered at the courage she had shown, and marveled at the way she had surprised us all. The love of a mother for her children is a miracle.

At a gentle breath of wind, the horses pulled their heads up, snorting and whinnying. They looked eager, sensitive to an urgency in the air. Edward patted them and let go. He stepped away, head bowed, though surely not in prayer. He seemed to have become a man possessed.

I could see Lucy battling to control her apprehension. Her resolve was strong, but I knew she must be in considerable pain. She was shivering.

Edward turned and looked toward her, then approached slowly. He knelt beside her, his gaze turned away from her defiant blazing eyes, and then removed the gag so she could speak. I thought I detected a pang of regret in his eyes. Perhaps he was confused at how he had allowed Hope to leave his house, how it was that Lucy had given herself up in Hope's place. Perhaps even his hardened heart had been moved by Lucy's courage and love. But if he had felt remorse it was only fleeting.

He looked to be considering something else, and then he leaned down and heaved her up. "How could you sacrifice yourself for my niece?" he asked quietly. "You're a burden, Lucy. I cannot escape with you. Oh, how I wish I was not the man I have become!"

He carried her back to the coach and placed her gently inside. The carriage rocked as he climbed in. He lifted her onto one of the seats. Then he swung shut the door, closing out the sound of the trees.

"I want you to understand me, before we are parted." He was smiling sadly, as if it weighed on him to have to speak to her like this. "When Ellen and I came away from India, we were adventurers, like you and your husband always wished you might be. But we achieved our dream, and you did not. When I began, I wanted only to employ the families who really needed help, the ones who'd struggled to keep out of the workhouse. Ellen and I felt as if we had truly helped Ormley." Edward stared out the window. "I wanted to find and employ only master weavers. I trusted your husband. He was a loyal servant to my family, to all of us."

Edward rubbed his mouth with the back of his hand. He was staring into the woodland, seemingly reliving his memories. "It was a glorious feeling," he said quietly. "Thank you for helping me believe, at least for a while, that I saved a man's family."

He fell silent. Lucy didn't move.

"But you know,' Edward said, his face now hard, "it was all of you that benefited. Dozens of families were rescued by my investment. I'm not sure anyone ever thanked us. I'm not sure you or Isaac, or either of your sons, ever thanked me. But they have all always wanted my fortune."

He climbed out of the carriage. "And so now I shall soon leave it to them, just as your husband wished me to. Shortly I shall die. The only final question is what is to be done about you. I had thought about demanding a ransom . . ."

Edward pulled a flintlock pistol from his cloak and turned it thoughtfully, over and over in his hands. "Of course, when Manny inherits my wealth, as he surely shall when he marries my niece" —Edward raised the gun and pointed it directly into Lucy's face— "it will be forever bitter."

He squinted, aiming the barrel of the gun. But the sound of men's voices and heavy footsteps crashing through the undergrowth stopped him from pulling the trigger. He fumbled with the gun in his haste to get out of the carriage. Half a dozen weavers were spread out and approaching through the trees.

Edward panicked at the sight of them, pointed the gun at Lucy again, and pulled the trigger. Through the smoke, I saw her fall back and slump over, blood spreading quickly over her dress.

At the sound of the gun, the weavers stopped. This gave Edward vital seconds he needed in order to escape. The carriage shook as he swung himself up onto the driver's seat and cracked the whip.

One of the weavers reached the coach, but just too late. It lurched forward and raced out through the trees, out into the moorland, faster as the horses picked up speed.

There was another jolt, and Lucy slipped from her seat. I could see her losing consciousness. Then with a sudden rush of excitement I knew that, at last, we were going to see each other, that I could finally keep my promise to come back for her.

I saw her spirit rising as the carriage clattered across the moorland, her life sacrificed for the sake of Manny and Hope, her old, worn-out body stretched out on the floor, jarring from the thud and the thump of the wheels.

Moving gracefully from the darkened carriage she saw me. I couldn't help laughing at her start of surprise, and in delight I rushed forward to greet and embrace her.

Nineteen

Meeting the Reeves

John looked utterly overwhelmed at the sight of his daughter. In spite of his brazen, sea-worn nature, he seemed unable to move or speak. But in that second, that magical moment of comprehending, Manny watched two lives connect before him. With a surge of pride, he saw joy pass over Hope's countenance. She broke down and wept—great, raking sobs of relief and delight.

It was only a second, perhaps even less, but Manny felt he had received a lifetime of understanding. He wanted to move but couldn't, so he stood watching, absorbing the blessed reunion of an estranged daughter with her father.

John was clearly both transfixed and alarmed at the sight of her, standing there in the doorway, her beautiful black hair tangled and bedraggled, her face dirty and streaked by tears. Her dress was splattered with mud, and though Manny wanted to know how she had escaped, it would be inappropriate to press her for details at this very moment. He shuddered at the thought of what she might have been through to get here. By the look of her, she had run all the way.

He forced himself not to ask about his mother. He did not want to intrude on this moment of reunion, no matter how greatly he desired to know why his mother had left Ormley with Edward Reeve.

It was hard to believe father and daughter had not seen each other in sixteen years. Hope looked unsure about what to do. Finally John moved, holding out his arms. Her look of uncertainty changed to grateful confidence, and she ran forward and embraced him.

John's whispered "I'm sorry" was almost inaudible, but Manny saw the contrition in his face.

Hope cried and laughed at the same time, every now and then exclaiming her delight. "I'm amazed. I don't believe it. It's a miracle." They held on to each other, each clasping the other like they might never let go.

When Hope looked up at Manny, he felt love sweep over him and renew every part of his being. And with it came something else—a feeling of divine acceptance. Like air at dawn, it lifted and cleansed and restored his mind and soul. At first he thought it was joy. But then, with a start of excitement, he realized it was more—this was the very Source from whence joy came. This renewing of strength was the healing love of the Master.

Manny would happily have kept his place in

the solicitor's room, watching and feeling the joy of reunion, basking in this sense of divine love. He knew now that the experience of joy was a gift from a loving Redeemer—his everlasting reason to love and follow Jesus.

But the peace was suddenly disturbed by frantic banging at the office door, followed by men's voices.

Sister Aitkin burst in. Behind her were several men from the village. "Manny," she said. "Your mother—they say she's away up on the moors. She's been shot."

"Mr. Shaw, hold on. Think of everyone's need," Mr. Thomas said sharply as Manny started to leave, but he was already pushing his way out of the solicitor's office. No one would prevent him from getting to his mam now.

⸺◦∞◦⸺

The men had arrived on horseback, but Manny had never been able to ride, so he sprinted all the way through town, the sound of Mr. Thomas's warning voice still ringing in his ears. His lungs burned as he sprinted back to the road that would take him across the moors to Ormley. If Reeve had been found hiding on his estate and had attempted to cross the moors, Manny knew the man would not be able to flee quickly. Unless Reeve doubled back and risked riding through the village—and there seemed little chance of that—the only other possible route would take him across the moors to Northwood. But there was also a good chance

Reeve would try to hide. Manny knew the police would station constables along the main highway to the village. He looked back only once and, to his surprise, saw that others had followed him. Constable Davidson was there, and Mr. Thomas, Hope, John, even Sister Aitkin. But Manny did not care whether they could keep up with him.

Though he had been completely disoriented upon hearing that his mother had run away with Reeve, Manny now realized what must have really happened. His mam had given up her freedom in order to rescue Hope and thus protect and preserve Manny's marriage, his future.

He knew Mr. Reeve was unpredictable and dangerous, and now as a fugitive from the law he would be as wily as a fox ahead of the hunt. Yet it wasn't preventing Reeve's escape that made Manny throw himself into the task of finding them. What he wanted more than anything now was to reach his mam, to give her the only gift he had left to give—the dignity of companionship.

It suddenly struck Manny that there was something remarkably familiar about this journey to Ormley. It was much like the one he had made on Monday, except in one particular. Days before, he had made a commitment to follow Jesus Christ. Now Manny's understanding of what that commitment meant had deepened.

He had felt so fortified by the unexpected feelings of peace and love in Mr. Thomas's office. He now sensed a much larger vision of the meaning of his life. In spite of not understanding death or the reason people suffered, Manny now knew there was a Divine Presence who cared for him—a truth he more clearly appreciated because this light had brought him out of confusion. And this light had brought back someone else. Hope.

Seeing her again, seeing her united with her father, having the blessing of her love—all of it gave Manny strength. Though he knew he must prove his faith throughout his life, he now believed with all his heart that there was a God, that there was life beyond the grave, that there was value and worth in the determination to live well. In the light of such awareness, he even felt an unexpected urgency to extend forgiveness to Reeve—a desire to love his enemy.

How, Manny wondered, could a man find the willingness to forgive, when he understood little of his enemy's heart and history? Was it possible or required that he might forgive even those whom he could not understand? What about those who showed no remorse?

Elder Armitage had said understanding was necessary to gain the compassion required to forgive, but it was impossible for Manny to understand Reeve. He had no way of gaining insight before the inevitable encounter.

His face streamed with sweat from the exertion of running so hard. He wasn't sure if he could maintain the pace, but the idea that Reeve might escape if he slackened his speed kept Manny going.

There was something else—an awareness that began to trouble him. His single-minded desire to help was now endangering the lives of those who had followed him. Mr. Thomas had been right to warn against hastiness. Armed and vicious, Reeve had nothing more to lose.

But it was inconceivable to turn back. Manny had an idea and gulped at the thought of it.

Manny flung open the Aldermans' stable door and nearly collapsed as he tried to regain his breath. For a moment he slumped against the wall, his legs weak and trembling, his hands shaking. His back was wet with sweat, his shirt drenched. He glanced up at the door. The shotgun had been above the lintel, but it wasn't there.

The musty stable was serenely quiet. He could have believed everything was normal—that Mr. Alderman was in the house reading, that Hope was waiting for Manny to visit, that he was still an Ormley weaver. He could almost imagine going home as he always had, to find Mam at the stove, the table set for tea.

Tiny flecks of hay spiraled in the light of the open doorway, and a thin layer of straw was scattered around the dirt floor. Where was the shotgun? Manny ran his hand over the door lintel where it had last been, then spun round to search, knocking against an old saddle. For another moment he stood rooted to the spot. The idea of confronting Reeve was ridiculous. But Manny looked again, searching the dimness.

It was there, in the corner of the stable. He felt his mouth turn dry at the thought of what he might be required to do. He picked up the gun and began to root through the sacks and tins in search of powder. The gun was no use without munitions. His hands shook, spilling gunpowder onto the floor as he loaded the rifle. He wasn't exactly sure how much to put in, but he thought he would need plenty. He had to find shot as well. He felt a rush of dread and desperation as he realized there was none. He threw down the gun in frustration but then had another idea.

He could use it to bluff—Reeve wouldn't know if it was loaded or not. It was dangerous, but it was the only plan Manny could think of. He staggered out of the stable and up toward the moor. Sunlight was creeping over the hills, the sky filled with a copper hue.

———

Manny stood holding the shotgun by the dry-stone wall, almost exactly where he and Mr. Alderman had been a few days earlier, when the old farmer had pointed out the tarn. The conversation seemed like a lifetime ago. Staring into the moorland, Manny scanned the horizon, searching the highway for any sight of the carriage. Since the moorland rose sharply from the village, a carriage would be slow and hidden until it reached the brow.

Overhead, a gull wheeled through the clouds and screeched its solitary call. Manny jumped over the wall and ran down the footpath to the track. Mr. Reeve would have to pass him here.

The track twisted steeply down into the valley, and there were several large boulders that would make the track hard for any large coach to navigate. If Manny was fast he could break down the dry-stone wall and create something of a blockade. He looked back and saw the others approaching. They could manage if they worked together. The roadblock would force the carriage to stop. If Reeve was brought down from the coach, they would be more equal.

Manny quickly hid the gun in a ditch. His plan might work if he moved swiftly. He placed the first stone and hurried back for more. Without a word, the group joined him, dashing to and from the wall, carrying stones, as many as they could, and a mound rose rapidly. It was substantial in size and would surely work.

Everyone rested briefly. They said nothing, clearly mindful of the imminent confrontation. Mr. Thomas was dabbing his brow. Hope and her father stood near, and Manny stepped close to her and took her hand. Constable Davidson had removed his hat and wore a half-pleased, half-apprehensive look. He spoke.

"I reckon someone ought to go to the village . . ."

Manny thought he heard the rattle of carriage wheels and the clatter of horses' hooves. He looked down at the village and wondered for a moment which of them would be the swiftest. But no one looked willing to leave. Sister Aitkin was the obvious choice, but it hardly seemed fair to ask her to go back to a village that had been rioting only an hour or so earlier. There was no time to press the point. But to Manny's relief, she volunteered.

"I don't know . . ." John said quickly.

Mr. Thomas stepped forward and said he could go.

Constable Davidson retook control. "Take Miss Alderman. I think it would be best if she went as well."

But Hope refused to go.

Constable Davidson looked as if he was trying to be calm, but he seemed frightened. There was no more time for arguing. "Right, right then," he said. "Don't move unless, or until, I ask for assistance."

"Sir, I . . ." Manny began. Now would be the right time to reveal the asset of the gun. But Constable Davidson was getting jumpy and brushed aside Manny's attempt to speak, urging them to hide.

The sound of horses was getting louder.

Manny took Hope by the arm and they ran to take cover in the ditch where he had hidden the shotgun. The solicitor and Sister Aitkin hurried away. Hope seemed confident, renewed, somehow beyond fear since the reunion with her father. Manny took her hand and she squeezed his gently, reassuringly. Constable Davidson and John had hidden themselves behind the barricade.

Everyone waited. The sound of horses whinnying and snorting announced the coach's arrival. Manny could imagine Mr. Reeve's look of disdain as he was forced to pull back on the reins.

The carriage had stopped. It was probably only a dozen yards away now. Manny reached out and gripped the shotgun. He had only to wait a few more moments. The policeman would confront Reeve any second now. Carefully and slowly, keeping himself hidden, Manny raised his head to watch Reeve's approach. The rise of the moorland and the thick heather all around them meant that if Manny kept very still he would remain unseen.

Mr. Reeve was putting down the reins, climbing from his seat. He paused for a moment at the side of the carriage and then walked forward to examine the obstruction.

Constable Davidson burst from his hiding place and scrambled forward, one hand holding his hat, the other reaching for his whistle. Reeve staggered back, pulling out two pistols, and leveled them at the policeman. Constable Davidson stopped, the whistle not quite to his mouth. From his look of dismay it was clear he had not expected Reeve to be armed with more than one gun. Before he could blow his whistle, Reeve shot. The policeman fell heavily and didn't get up.

Mr. Reeve took a half step back to the carriage, glancing around nervously. There was an anxious pause while those who were hiding waited to see if Constable Davidson would move. Then John rose from his hiding place. The initial look of surprise on Edward Reeve's face was replaced by derision. "Hello, Brother," he said. "Welcome home."

They stood facing each other, having been strangers for sixteen years. Neither spoke. After what seemed an eternity, though it must only have been seconds, John took a step toward his brother, his hands raised to show he was unarmed. Edward raised his gun and pulled back the hammer.

Manny had been so focused on this confrontation that he hadn't realized Hope was watching. As soon as Edward raised the gun, she made a sudden dash forward, clearly intent on going to her father's side. Manny tried to stop her, but she pulled away from him and ran down to stand with her father.

Clenching his teeth, his heart pounding, Manny pulled the shotgun to his shoulder and stood up, pointing it at Mr. Reeve. Visibly shaken, the man retreated to the side of the carriage. For a moment he stood, one hand holding tight to the side of the coach, the other waving the pistol at each of his assailants in turn.

"Put your gun down," Manny called.

Mr. Reeve wore a crazed smile. "I see. Very good. I cannot kill three of you. Do you propose to shoot me now, Shaw, or would you like to see my hanging?"

"Keep your tongue to yourself, fraud," John shouted. He made to move forward, but Hope stepped in front of him and caught his arm.

Manny knew what she must be thinking. She was right. John's death would gain nothing.

Edward Reeve's face flushed crimson. "Oh no, I don't think so, Brother. You're the fraud—you're the coward."

"You don't deceive us no more," Manny shouted. He nodded in the direction of the village. "They'll all be coming."

Edward laughed. Then without warning he lurched forward and grabbed Hope before anyone else could move. He backed away slowly, the pistol pressed to her head.

Manny turned cold. He moved a step closer, the gun stock pressed against his face, the wind ruffling his hair. He knew he couldn't bluff much longer. He only had seconds before Edward realized the shotgun wasn't loaded.

The mill owner began to laugh, and Manny lowered the shotgun. Laughing still and holding fast to Hope, Edward flung open the carriage door and stepped away so Manny could see inside.

Twenty

One Perfect Freedom

Manny saw his mam's body sprawled on the floor of the carriage, her head thrown back, glazed eyes staring up blankly. Blood pooled on the carriage floor. He was shocked at the sight of her, outraged at the sight of her indignity—mouth gagged, hands and feet tied.

"I've still one shot," Reeve said dangerously. Sixteen years of deceit was now taking its toll as madness poured out of him at a furious pace, the beginning of his own desperate death throes. He waved the pistol at John. "Move back. Move back, I say!"

Manny bent down slowly, placing the rifle on the ground. "Don't hurt her, Reeve," he said, just about holding his voice together. "For her sake and mine, don't shoot her." They had very little time left. "Don't . . . you can't. She's your niece! You can't . . ."

But Reeve's eyes had a kind of vacant wildness. He was beyond reason, suddenly unreachable.

There was no flinging of arms, no shouting or screaming. Just intent.

In Manny's mind, everything became very still, very quiet. He moved through his thoughts with a new determination, concentrating on the position and direction of Reeve's gun, trying to feel his way into a solution. Hope's life hung by a thread. There was nothing Manny could do. If he moved, she would be shot.

"I won't leave you, Hope," he said.

"Be quiet, Shaw," Edward Reeve snapped.

"John came back to Ormley," Manny continued, "to put things right. He's a good man, a brave man."

It came to Manny that he must keep the conversation going. Help would come—in fact, it might arrive at any minute.

But John made a sudden movement, as if to help Hope. Edward was just as quick, dragging her back almost into the carriage.

Then Constable Davidson groaned.

They all looked down at him. Edward was the first to react. "Take him to the village," he sneered. He was addressing John but nodded toward the constable. "Take him to the village to get treated." When John hesitated, Edward pressed the gun harder against Hope's head, and Manny saw her wince. "Do it, John." A cruel smile flickered on Reeve's face. "It's only right—it's what Isaac did for you."

Manny knew John had no choice. Only the possibility that it might help his daughter seemed to persuade him to do as Edward asked. John raised a trembling finger and stabbed it toward his brother's face. "If you so much as harm a hair of her head, Edward," he spat. He heaved the policeman up and carried him away, obviously struggling under the weight.

Once John was out of sight, Edward looked at Manny. "Tie her up." He gestured to a coil of rope on the roof of the carriage.

Like John, Manny hesitated. Edward cocked the pistol's hammer. Before Manny could move, Hope began to struggle. Suddenly he knew what she was doing.

"No, Hope," Manny pleaded. He ran forward, trying to stop her. Edward swung the pistol, hitting him with the barrel of the gun.

Hope seemed to hesitate for a moment. Then, with a look of resolve, she bit Edward's hand. In one swift action she was flung into the carriage.

"No!" Manny shouted. "Don't—"

Wood and glass splintered over the highway as the gun went off, and Hope fell back inside the carriage. The horses reared and then bolted, dragging the carriage over the rocks and the boulders. The coach was thrown onto its side, and unable to pull it farther, the horses were forced to stop.

Manny grabbed the rifle and swung it, but Edward ducked out of the way and then tripped, dropping the pistol. It clattered over the stones and came to rest on the other side of the road. They dived together, both trying to wrestle the other back. Pushing Edward away, Manny fell, just short of the gun. He twisted round, trying to get to his feet, but Edward wrenched him back and grabbed his face, holding him down on the ground. He struggled to inhale as Edward pressed down on his throat.

Manny wriggled desperately and slipped free, then leaned back and punched the mill owner in the mouth. He felt the sting of teeth on his fist, felt Edward fall away from him. Manny grasped the shotgun and swiftly got up, holding it like a club. He could smell the mill, the rope, the twine, the dust; he could see the dark room and Mr. Reeve standing close to him, could hear the faintly mocking tone of the mill master's voice. "Your mother will thank you to keep silent." Manny felt a knot at the base of his stomach, his longing to cry, or to scream, just wanting to cover his embarrassment, his shame— naked to the laughing, the pointing.

He looked at the upturned carriage, the horses, the moorland, and it felt like all of it was pulling away and then racing back. The carriage lay on its side, one of the wheels still turning, the horses rearing and neighing.

But Edward Reeve's face was ashen. He was kneeling on the ground, looking horrified, as if suddenly realizing what he had done. He knelt there, rocking, inconsolable, back and forth like a child, sobbing. When he finally looked up at Manny, all of the hate, all of the insanity and cruelty had gone. There was only grief and regret and sorrow, a man aware, finally coming to himself. For the first time in his life, Manny saw Reeve full of remorse.

He was begging forgiveness. Manny knew it— knew Reeve was broken, and he saw what was now being offered. This was the beginning of justice—for all of the pain, all of the lies, all the unfairness and crime. This was a beginning of justice for his mam's suffering, for his dad's betrayal, and for Will's death. And it was justice for Hope.

Manny heard the shouts and the sound of men and women approaching from the village. He knew what he must do. Breathing slowly, and then stepping away, he threw the shotgun down.

Reeve looked afraid and got up jerkily, brushing pointlessly at the mud on his trousers. There were more shouts, and Manny saw a large police officer emerge at the brow of the hill, running at speed toward them. Reeve looked at the upturned carriage and then began to back away. There were still more shouts and then a shrill police whistle.

Crows scattered from the trees, clapping their wings, cawing as they fled. For a moment, Mr. Reeve stood stock still as if transfixed by the arrival of the law and bewildered by it all. Then, as if he finally saw that he was no longer part of the village, he turned and fled.

He ran stupidly, his cloak billowing out and flapping behind him, his arms flailing as he ran across the open expanse. But he had nowhere to go, and Manny watched the constables pursue him. Reeve's carefully preserved façade, like mist before the rising sun, had vanished.

Turning back toward the carriage, Manny paused and tried to catch his breath, concerned at what else he must see. He was unable to let anyone else take care of his loved ones, yet afraid to retrieve them himself, distraught at the thought of being witness to their dead bodies. Against his will, he stepped nearer. As he did so, someone called his name.

It was Hope. In a daze, scarcely able to believe she was yet alive, Manny climbed over the upturned vehicle and peered into the half-lit carriage. Hope looked up at him and managed a fleeting smile. Apart from a graze on her cheek, the bullet had not harmed her. Manny could hardly breathe.

Beside her lay his mam, stretched out, her face white. Yet Hope looked intent and beckoned him to join her. Hardly daring to believe what he thought she might mean, he lowered himself into the carriage and then knelt beside her. As he did so his mam stirred and Manny saw she was not dead.

Her eyes flickered as he held her hand. Then, gently, as he had done for Will, Manny placed his coat under her head as a makeshift pillow. The wound from the gunshot was deep and severe. He simply could not grasp how his mam had escaped death. It was a miracle. And as he gazed at her, trying desperately to understand, he felt a gradually building peace, until he knew with all his heart that hosts of angels were all around them. His mam would live. They had, all of them, lived.

And then suddenly, Manny and Hope were laughing and crying, laughing and crying for joy, holding tight to each other and wrapped in each other's arms. In that moment, when they meant never to let go, a conviction came over Manny with such force that he gasped in wonder. From the top of his head to the soles of his feet, he knew he would never again be separated from Hope. Always and forever they would be one, throughout his lifetime and after the grave. Grateful and awestruck, he looked into her eyes, heard the beating of her heart in her breath, felt the powerful unspoken desire they shared. And gently, softly at first, then with increasing intent, they joyfully kissed.

When Manny finally climbed out of the carriage with Hope, a hushed crowd of villagers had gathered a short distance away. Those at the front looked unsure about coming closer, holding others back as well. They were silent and watchful, clearly affected by the sight of the upturned coach and the arrest of Mr. Reeve.

Mr. Thomas stood at the front of them, where he had been reasoning with them to remain where they were, confirming the appropriateness of showing respect. Then a man shouted, and Manny saw John break from the crowd and come rushing toward them. He looked like a man whose life had just been renewed—a great, unspeakable weight lifted from his heart. Finally liberated, he took his daughter in his powerful arms and held her tight. Manny stood by, glad for her good fortune, sharing in her delight.

Quickly though, he began to be aware of the difference, struggling with the fact that he was only witness to this encompassing parental love. He turned away, bending down to help his mam, unable to look her in the eye.

He wasn't even sure what to say to her. He knew he must seek forgiveness for the suffering inadvertently brought upon her, for the separation from Will, for the grief she would feel over his untimely death. If only there was something Manny could say that might lift her, something to comfort them both.

He tried to speak but stopped at the look on his mam's face—a look he hadn't seen for as long as he could remember, a look absent since his Dad had died.

She looked at peace, profoundly at peace. And she was smiling.

"Mam, I . . ."

"Hush, child."

With those two simple words came relief. For the first time in sixteen years, Manny allowed himself to feel like the child he had never been able to be.

"I'm sorry," he said. "If I'd only—"

"Manny," his mam said. She said it soberly, but he was startled again to detect the joy in her voice, the excitement. "Manny, I've seen your dad. There's a life after death. Will isn't gone."

She was smiling now, no doubt at the look of wonder and awe Manny felt spreading all over his face.

"Listen to me," she repeated. "I've seen your father. I've spent time with Isaac. There's work for all of us to do."

───⟨∞⟩───

Wood pigeons were calling from the trees, and above the ridge of burnt rock at the brow of the hill, a shaft of sunlight slipped through the cloud, then swept along the moorland road. It might almost have been the day of the baptisms again.

I knew Manny felt this sense of newness, and for a moment we were of one mind. I was filled with light, filled with gratitude for my son's courage and coming of age. Most of all, I gave thanks that his future included Hope. I sang a rejoicing song of love as I watched them pass happily over the fields. Then I stood silent, reverent, as the sky was changed to a sea of beings—the presence of angels, spirits of the dead, filling the air around me, around us. I thought also of those yet to be born who might be rejoicing in this day of renewed opportunity.

As I saw those who were past, I wished Manny could see his posterity—all of those who were destined now to benefit from his courage to live his conviction. I hoped he would always feel the peace that was breathing life into the once-barren valley.

Whatever else he felt or perceived, I prayed that just as Mary, the mother of Jesus, Manny would keep these sacred things and ponder them in his heart.

I saw Hope smiling and Manny take hold of her, sweeping her up in his arms. Then together they turned and faced the waiting villagers. Somewhere toward the back of the gathered crowd, someone began to clap, and gradually more and more joined in until the sound of the clapping and cheering echoed across the valley.

I watched them all leave and knew I must accompany them no longer. Wishing I could follow and yet knowing I must not, I prayed I had done enough for my family's salvation. I knew Manny would see to my baptism. I prayed the truth Jesus taught would keep us all free.

How grateful I was to be able to keep my promise to Lucy. Now I would seek to go to Will.

I watched the crowd of weavers parting like the Red Sea itself, making way for Manny and Hope. He looked back just once. But it was with a look of knowledge and not doubt that he looked—a look of wisdom, of deep appreciation—and I knew he realized I was saying goodbye, until some distant reunion.

Turning away, he held fast to Hope's hand, and together they passed through the crowd to begin their way along the bridle path, and on to the village and home.

Author's Note

My interest in the nineteenth-century British LDS experience probably goes back further than I realize. But in 2002 I began to develop a story that could examine the experience of a young man's conversion to Mormonism. In doing this I wondered what might have become of those many actual people who, experiencing the spirit of the Restoration during that first LDS mission, were not initially baptized. What unseen consequences might have taken place in the hearts and lives of the thousands of men, women, and children who heard the gospel message but did not join the Church?

In the end, what I think I have achieved in *Hope* is a narrative that concentrates on the human experience of conversion to Christ. To that end, this book is best seen as an allegory rather than as a faithful history of actual events. Nevertheless, the locations and landscapes sketched out in the novel are inspired and informed by the area where I live—which is South Lancashire, some ten miles or so from Preston and within the same ward boundaries that include the village of Eccleston, an area from which the first English immigrant converts came.

I live in Chorley, a Lancashire market town in Northwest England. Bordering the West Pennine moors, Chorley dates back over five hundred years and is home to the Preston England Temple. The moorland is a bleak and rugged but beautiful place, a landscape that must appear much the way the first seven missionaries saw it. Chorley is also close to Downham and Chatburn, villages in which Heber C. Kimball famously preached in the early Victorian period.

Since *Hope* is a work of my imagination and was only inspired by real places and events, there is no reason to believe that the events in the story actually happened, except, of course, for the energetic arrival of those first missionaries in 1837 and the dramatic effect on generations to come. During my university research, my intention was to more fully grasp the nature and meaning of Latter-day Saint religious commitment in the nineteenth century—to seek to more fully grasp the viewpoints and attitudes that shaped their faith. I have come to appreciate just how alike we are to them. The same expansive doctrines inspire us today, delivered under the direction of the same dedicated priesthood authority and apostolic leadership. As Latter-day Saints, our relationship to and with the rest of the world is defined by our unique sense of identity—that we belong to the restored Church, approved and sanctioned by God Himself, ordained to spearhead the gathering of Israel. Our spiritual experiences, testimonies, and conversion to Christ are the same today as they were in the nineteenth century. Discipleship is still demanding, refining, and exhilarating, and just as vital today as it was then.

Ultimately, this piece of writing is an attempt to plot the journey of faith and explore the meaning of conversion. The setting is Northwest England, the time mid-Victorian Britain. Yet, as the Book of Mormon teaches, "time only is measured unto men," and the human need for Christ is eternal.

Finally, the words I have presumed to put into Elder Fielding's mouth are my invention; I can only hope they do him justice.

On the following pages, I have included a selection of key sources that may be helpful to readers interested in discovering more about the spiritual lives of British and, for that matter, American LDS converts in the nineteenth century.

Sources

Though there are masses of sources on the history of the Latter-day Saints, the following selection provides a good place to begin. Happy researching!

Primary Sources

Book of Mormon, The. Salt Lake City, Utah: The Church of Jesus Christ of Latter-day Saints, 1989. Originally published in 1830.

Dickens, Charles. *The Uncommercial Traveller and Reprinted Pieces etc.* London: Oxford University Press, 1958.

Doctrine and Covenants, The. Salt Lake City, Utah: The Church of Jesus Christ of Latter-day Saints, 1989. Originally published in 1833 as A Book of Commandments.

Hewitson, Anthony. *History of Preston.* Preston, England: Preston Chronicle, 1883.

———. *Our Churches and Chapels Their Parsons, Priests & Congregations; being a Critical and Historical account of every place of worship in Preston.* Preston, England: Preston Chronicle, 1869 (reprint).

Holy Bible, The. Authorized King James Version, with explanatory notes and cross-references to the standard works of The Church of Jesus Christ of Latter-day Saints. Salt Lake City, Utah: The Church of Jesus Christ of Latter-day Saints, 1989.

Mormon Immigration Index. FamilySearch. org. Includes various letter, diary extracts, autobiographical sketches, and voyage information of emigrants, covering the years 1840 through 1890, usually in extract form. Salt Lake City, Utah: The Church of Jesus Christ of Latter-day Saints, 2000.

Pearl of Great Price, The. Salt Lake City, Utah: The Church of Jesus Christ of Latter-day Saints, 1989. A version was originally published in 1851; see introductory note in the 1989 edition.

Preston Chronicle, 20 Jan. 1838.

Smith, E.R.S. *Biography and Family Record of Lorenzo Snow, One of the Twelve Apostles of The Church of Church of Jesus Christ of Latter-day Saints.* Salt Lake City, Utah, Deseret News, 1884. The Church of Jesus Christ of Latter-day Saints. Salt Lake City, Utah: 1999 (facsimile reprint).

Smith, Joseph. *Lectures on Faith: Delivered to the School of the Prophets in Kirtland, Ohio, 1834–35.* Salt Lake City, Utah: Deseret Book Company, 1985. Originally published in 1835.

Smith, Joseph. *Teachings of the Prophet Joseph Smith.* Comp. Joseph Fielding Smith. Salt Lake City, Utah: Deseret Book, 1976.

The Times, 6 Jan. 1854. This is an extensive supplement to a religious census carried out in England in 1851. Also, *The Times* entries "Mormon," "Mormonism," and "Mormonite" are accessible via the Palmers Index to *The Times* and provide insight into Victorian beliefs and opinions about the Mormon Church.

Thompson David M., ed. *Nonconformity in the Nineteenth Century.* London: Routledge & Kegan Paul, 1972.

Secondary Sources

Allen, James B., Ronald K. Esplin, and David J. Whittaker. *Men with a Mission 1837–1841: The Quorum of the Twelve Apostles in the British Isles.* Salt Lake City, Utah: Deseret Book Company, 1992.

Arrington, Leonard J. *Brigham Young: American Moses.* New York: Alfred Knopf, 1985.

Arrington, Leonard J., and Davis Bitton. *The Mormon Experience: A History of the Latter-day Saints.* New York: Vintage Books, 1980. Originally published by Alfred Knopf, 1979.

Best, Geoffrey. *Mid-Victorian Britain 1851–1875.* London: Fontana Press, 1979.

Bloxham V. Ben, James R. Moss, and Larry C. Porter, eds. *Truth Will Prevail: The Rise of The Church of Jesus Christ of Latter-day Saints in the British Isles, 1837–1987.* Cambridge, United Kingdom: Cambridge University Press, 1987.

Bushman, Richard L. *Joseph Smith and the Beginnings of Mormonism.* Champaign, Illinois: University of Illinois Press, 1984.

Chadwick, Owen. *The Victorian Church, Part I.* Second edition. London: Adam and Charles, 1970.

———, *The Victorian Church, Part II.* London: Adam & Charles Black, 1970.

Church History in the Fulness of Times. Salt Lake City, Utah: The Church of Jesus Christ of Latter-day Saints, 1989.

Davies, Douglas J. *An Introduction to Mormonism.* Cambridge, United Kingdom: Cambridge University Press, 2003.

Gabbacia, Donna R. *Immigration and American Diversity: A Social and Cultural History.* Oxford, United Kingdom: Blackwell Publishers, 2002.

Gibbons, Frances M. *Dynamic Disciples, Prophets of God: Life Stories of the Presidents of The Church of Jesus Christ of Latter-day Saints.* Salt Lake City, Utah, Deseret Book Company, 1996.

Gilley, Sheridan, and W. J. Sheils, eds. *A History of Religion in Britain Practice and Belief from Pre-Roman Times to the Present.* Oxford, United Kingdom: Blackwell Publishers, 1994.

Houghton, Walter E. *The Victorian Frame of Mind, 1830–1870.* Published for Wellesley College, New Haven and London. New Haven, Connecticut: Yale University Press, 1957.

Inglis, K.S. *Churches and the Working Class in Victorian England.* London: Routledge and Kenyan Paul; and Toronto: University of Toronto Press. 1963.

Jensen, Richard L. and Thorp Malcolm R, eds. *Mormons in Early Victorian Britain.* Salt Lake City, Utah: University of Utah Press, 1989.

Kimball, Stanley B. *Heber C. Kimball.* Champaign, Illinois: University of Illinois Press, 1981.

Ludlow, Daniel H. ed. *Encyclopedia of Mormonism.* 4 vols. New York: Macmillan, 1992.

Madsen, Truman G. *Joseph Smith the Prophet*. Salt Lake City, Utah: Bookcraft, 1989.

Nightingale, Benjamin. *Lancashire Nonconformity, or Sketches, Historical & Descriptive of the Congregational and Old Presbyterian Churches in the County*. London: John Heywood, circa 1891.

Richards, LeGrand. *A Marvelous Work and a Wonder*. Salt Lake City, Utah: Deseret Book Company, 1976.

Shipps, Jan. *Mormonism: The Story of a New Religious Tradition*. Champaign, Illinois: University of Illinois Press, 1985.

Swinton, Heidi S. *American Prophet: The Story of Joseph Smith*. Based on the documentary by Lee Groberg. Salt Lake City, Utah: Shadow Mountain, 1999.

Taylor, P.A.M. *Expectations Westward: The Mormons and the Emigration of Their British Converts in the Nineteenth Century*. Edinburgh and London: Oliver & Boyd, 1965.

Thompson, E.P. *The Making of the English Working Class*. New York: Penguin Books, 1963.

Whitney, Orson F. *Life of Heber C. Kimball*. Salt Lake City, Utah: Juvenile Instructor (Deseret Book Company), 1888.

For a pleasant, accessible documentary about early LDS missionaries in the United Kingdom, watch *Faith in Their Footsteps: The First Apostles in Great Britain*. Really committed researchers might want to visit www.ldstours.co.uk or www.ldsbritain.blogspot.co.uk.

About the Author

S. J. (Seth) Wilkins lives close to the village from which the first British LDS immigrants left for America, and close to the beautiful but rugged west Pennine moors which inspired Hope's setting. He taught at the Preston England Missionary Training Centre between 1999 and 2002, able to look out on the same moorland the early missionaries must have seen after they first arrived in England. Seth appeared as Heber C. Kimball in the 2009 documentary *Faith in Their Footsteps* and has researched extensively at the University of Lancaster, graduating with masters of arts degrees in history and creative writing. In 2013, following almost six years in LDS retailing, he began training as a teacher.

To learn more about *Hope,* or to contact Seth, please visit http://musingona.blogspot.com.